"Then why are you here." Zander said, ignoring her dizzying proximity and the scent he apparently hadn't forgotten.

"Is there a problem with the payment of your invoice?" he asked.

"No."

"Do you have some other business involving my company?"

"No."

"Are you in trouble?"

"Not exactly."

"I don't have time for riddles," he said, his surging frustration at the way Mia was addling his brain *finally* igniting some strength of character. "And I fail to see anything else we might have to discuss, so if you'll excuse me, I have somewhere else to be."

Wrenching himself away from her compelling gaze, Zander turned on his heel, intending to round the screen and head for the exit, practically tasting fresh air and freedom, only to come to an abrupt stop when she spoke, her words flying through the space and landing on him like darts.

"I'm pregnant."

Lucy King spent her adolescence lost in the glamorous and exciting world of Harlequin when she really ought to have been paying attention to her teachers. But as she couldn't live in a dreamworld forever, she eventually acquired a degree in languages and an eclectic collection of jobs. After a decade in southwest Spain, Lucy now lives with her young family in Wiltshire, England. When not writing or trying to think up new and innovative things to do with mince, she spends her time reading, failing to finish cryptic crosswords and dreaming of the golden beaches of Andalusia.

Books by Lucy King

Harlequin Presents

Stranded with My Forbidden Billionaire

Heirs to a Greek Empire

Virgin's Night with the Greek

Lost Sons of Argentina

The Secrets She Must Tell
Invitation from the Venetian Billionaire
The Billionaire without Rules

Passionately Ever After...

Undone by Her Ultra-Rich Boss

Passion in Paradise

A Scandal Made in London

Visit the Author Profile page
at Harlequin.com for more titles.

Lucy King

———

A CHRISTMAS CONSEQUENCE FOR THE GREEK

HARLEQUIN®
PRESENTS™

Recycling programs
for this product may
not exist in your area.

ISBN-13: 978-1-335-59208-8

A Christmas Consequence for the Greek

Copyright © 2023 by Lucy King

Harlequin Enterprises ULC
22 Adelaide St. West, 41st Floor
Toronto, Ontario M5H 4E3, Canada
www.Harlequin.com

Printed in U.S.A.

A CHRISTMAS CONSEQUENCE FOR THE GREEK

CHAPTER ONE

'I KNOW YOU have an aversion to mixing business with pleasure,' Zander Stanhope murmured into Mia Halliday's ear as she handed him a coupe glass filled with raspberry and champagne posset and resisted the ever-present urge to climb him like a tree, 'because you've mentioned it countless times over the last four months. But as of two a.m. tonight, when this club closes and the party's over, you no longer work for me. Just a thought.'

With a smouldering smile, his eyes glinting wickedly, Zander straightened and turned to stride off, all towering height, broad shoulders and athletic grace. Mia just stood there and stared at his retreating figure, struck dumb by his observation and frozen to the spot between a ball-juggling clown and an impossibly bendy fire-eater.

Her mind raced as she watched him sink

onto a purple velvet banquette between two of his siblings and begin to make quick work of the dessert. Her heart pounded and her blood heated as his words and their implication sank in.

Just a thought.

The man was a menace, she reflected, pulling herself together to navigate the obstacle course of scantily clad dancers atop podiums, magicians, acrobats, feathers and bubbles that led from louche sensuality to the welcome clinical soullessness of the kitchen. A tall, dark, gorgeous menace.

They'd met back in June, shortly after he'd contacted her to request her catering services at the party he was throwing to celebrate his thirty-fifth birthday.

Initially, she'd thought the call some kind of bizarre prank because why would a half-Greek, half-British shipping and banking tycoon who regularly graced the pages of both the financial and tabloid press be calling *her*? Halliday Catering was growing and gaining a reputation for being fresh and innovative, certainly, but it did not yet cater to members of the elite world in which he operated.

Once she'd got over her shock and disbelief, she'd been ridiculously flattered when he'd told her that he'd read an article about her in a magazine and had instantly determined that no one else would do. She'd fizzled with excitement at the realisation that his influence might lead to a stampede of his well-heeled friends and acquaintances to her door, thereby securing the future of her business.

Because she tended to liaise with clients remotely in the early stages of planning an event, she never imagined that two days later he'd turn up at her premises on an industrial estate in east London to discuss the menu *in person*. At no point had she considered that, having done so, he'd bowl her over so thoroughly with his devastating looks and powerful presence that, from that point on, all she'd be able to think about when it came to him was sex.

Inconveniently, however, that was precisely what had happened.

Without so much as a text to inform her of his intentions, he'd strolled into her unit that afternoon and every one of her senses had switched to high alert. She'd instinctively looked up and then shot to her feet, as if her computer had given her an electric shock. She'd placed her hand in his and gazed dazedly into eyes the colour of cocoa while he'd introduced himself in deep faintly accented tones that oozed through her like warm golden syrup, and she'd been immediately gripped by an attraction that had turned out to be fierce and unrelenting.

In the weeks that followed, whenever an email dropped into her inbox, her heart skipped a beat. At the sight of his name flashing up on her phone her mouth dried and her head swam. In preparation for each of their three working lunches, she'd taken extra care with her clothes and make-up, even as she'd berated herself for her vanity.

It hadn't helped that he'd made no secret of his attraction to her, which she really couldn't fathom when he'd dated virtually every super-model and socialite on the planet. However, he spoke to her as if she were the only woman in existence and ran his gaze over her body as if mentally undressing her. The intensity of his attention left her dazed and breathless and in-creasingly on the brink of doing the job for him.

But despite the charm he wielded like a weapon and the slow sexy smile he deployed to dazzling effect, with superhuman effort, Mia had held out. She'd refused his invitation to dinner, even saying no to a drink, and become immune to the teasing gleam in his eye. She'd ignored the knowing air that suggested he en-joyed testing her willpower by subtly laying

siege to her defences and had convinced herself that the flare of emotion she'd caught in his
expression when she'd turned him down must
have been disbelief because in a player like him
it couldn't possibly have been hurt.

She would not jeopardise this opportunity to
get her name out there by caving in to base desires and fanciful sentimentality and potentially
messing up such an important job. She needed
to stay focused and on track if she wanted her
company to become number one in its field.
To achieve the financial and environmental security she'd lacked as a child—a child who'd
regularly missed school to care for her increasingly sick mother, a child who'd kept secrets
and lived in fear of being ripped away by social
services from everything she'd ever known—
she had to remain strong.

And she had.

Until he'd murmured those words in her ear
just now and sent her into a spin.

Because he had a point.

She'd been so busy pouring her efforts into
making the food at this party new and exciting, perfect and memorable, it hadn't occurred
to her that, once the event was over, the business she had with him would be concluded,
and she'd be free to act on the desire that had

clawed away at her for so long. Put there by a man who tormented her day and night, a man she wanted beyond reason and could, in theory, soon have. It was the only thought in her head.

So what was she going to do about it? she wondered, heart thumping as she removed a crate of chocolate truffles from the fridge and handed it to Hattie, her friend, her second-in-command and her only directly employed member of staff, who was charged with the task of arranging them on platters. Was that even a question that needed debate?

No.

She'd never experienced attraction like it and couldn't remember the last time she'd let her hair down. Her last disaster of a relationship, which in hindsight had been more hard work than anything else, had ended two years ago and since then she'd been so focused on the business and achieving the goals she'd had for ever, she hadn't been on so much as a date.

Besides, it wasn't as if she was after a relationship with him, which would have given her pause for thought. She knew what he was. She read the papers and had witnessed in person the skill with which he fielded the myriad personal phone calls he received.

His cavalier attitude towards women—

wholly incompatible with her longing for a solid relationship that would provide the security and love she craved as a result of her emotionally tumultuous upbringing—was well-documented. But while he possessed an infamous reputation as a ruthless heartbreaker, he would never break *her* heart. She wouldn't give him the chance. She had no desire to change him. She wasn't stupid. Once upon a time she'd had an unfortunate tendency to expect more from the men she dated than they were willing to give, but not any longer.

And yes, she'd sensed a barely leashed energy in him and had occasionally caught a bleakness in his gaze when it wasn't gleaming wickedly, which suggested that beneath the super cool playboy exterior troubled waters flowed, but of what relevance was that? She wouldn't be swimming in them for long. Even if they *had* shared more than just chemistry, Christmas was coming and she'd soon be busier than ever.

She'd worried that Zander had the ability to derail her ambitions. She'd feared messing this job up if she weakened and wasted the opportunity to strengthen her reputation and expand her company. But from a catering point of view, the event had been a triumph. Her food had been devoured. She'd handed out so many business cards she'd have to order more.

So what was stopping her from celebrating her success with one night of the hot sex she and Zander had both wanted for months?

Absolutely nothing.

From his sprawled position on the plush padded banquette, Zander toyed with a glass of vintage champagne and tracked Mia through narrowed eyes as she expertly weaved a path through guests and performers, distributing after-dinner confectionery.

If he'd known how tough a nut she was going to be to crack, he'd have turned the page on the article that had caught his attention when he'd been idly flicking through the magazine he'd encountered on the jet that had been flying him from San Francisco to Tokyo. He would never have lingered on the accompanying image and carelessly indulged the spike of interest he'd experienced at the arresting combination of red-gold hair and light blue eyes. He'd have gone with the club's own catering team instead of paying them a hefty sum to step aside for hers and saved himself a whole lot of trouble.

Four months of burning, unassuaged need he'd suffered. Four months of rejection both overt and implied, of fitful sleep and frustration unlike anything he'd ever known. Had Mia been a business partner or rival, a sister, an acquaintance or pretty much anyone else, he would have admired her unshakeable resolve. Because she was someone he'd badly wanted to take to bed for weeks, he could not.

'Why are you scowling at the caterer?'

In response to Thalia's question, dryly delivered in Greek, Zander instantly cleared his expression. He pasted on a languid smile instead and swung his attention to his younger sister. 'The risotto was on the gritty side, didn't you think?' he drawled, annoyed that he'd let his irritation show. 'And how original a flavour, really, is pea and mint?'

Thalia rolled her eyes and batted him on the arm. 'All the food was excellent, as you well know. I heard amazing things about the salmon, and the chicken katsu curry was the best I've ever tasted. Little bowls of heaven,' she said on a contented sigh. 'Those circus-themed canapés were exquisite and don't get me started on the dessert. This is an awesome party, even if I did nearly get taken out by a trapeze. Everyone's having a great time. Apart from you.' She stopped and frowned, then leaned in to study him a fraction more intently. 'Why the face of thunder, Zan? Selene's not here to cause a scene, and it can't seriously be the caterer, so what's really up? Is it the business? Are you ill? What?'

Ostensibly, it *was* the caterer. He wasn't ill and Stanhope Kallis, the family banking and shipping empire of which he'd been CEO since his elder brother Leo had resigned from the post six years ago, was going from strength to strength under his leadership. He couldn't care less that Selene—his scandalous, self-absorbed mother—hadn't even responded to the invitation he'd sent her, let alone shown up tonight. When had she ever been interested in him or what he was doing, unless it directly related to the dividends she lived off? Sure, the ease with which his five siblings and their various other halves interacted, something he'd never been able to either understand or emulate, roiled his stomach but that was nothing new.

Mia's attitude towards him was the superficial cause of his brooding tension but as for what was *really* up, he hadn't a clue. Why did her obstinacy bother him so much that he felt the constant urge to challenge it? Why couldn't he accept that she didn't want to act on the obvious chemistry they shared, and move on? Why had he felt so driven to hire her in the first place and why hadn't he taken a step back from the arrangements the minute he'd realised he was fighting a battle he likely wouldn't win?

The unanswerable nature of these questions, which had recently started taking up so much space in his head, set him on edge. His legendary focus was shot. He was unusually plagued by doubt. The suspicion that she could somehow see through his armour into the pit where his many flaws lurked crawled beneath his skin. Worse, somewhere deep inside, he could feel the unacceptable stir of emotions that he'd kept under lock and key for almost three decades.

He hadn't been so hurled off-balance by a woman since his one and only attempt at a relationship at the age of nineteen, which had been a never-to-be-repeated fiasco, and frankly, he'd had enough. Of all of it.

He was done with obsessing over Mia's refusal to have dinner with him. She'd said no and that was fine. He didn't know why it bothered him so much. Because it had never happened before? Because he might have misread the signs and could therefore be losing his touch? Whatever was going on, he was sick of the inexplicable, unsettling effect she had on him. She wasn't *that* attractive. He could think of a hundred women more beautiful and intriguing than her. This unrequited…hankering…he had for her was ridiculous. It was a complete waste of his time and, now he thought about it, wholly unacceptable.

How could he have forgotten the lessons he'd learned from his parents as a kid—that wanting things he couldn't have never went well and that indulging sentiment only led to pain and confusion? Since when had he been so weak? And so what if he *had* crashed and burned? It happened. Apparently.

Mia might not want him, but there were plenty of women who did. Some of them were here, in fact. He could find the physical release he craved with any one of them. They wouldn't resist him. They'd be delighted with an invitation to dinner or drinks or something else entirely. Wasn't that why they stayed in touch?

'You know what?' he said to Thalia, firmly shoving Mia out of his mind once and for all, the way he should have done weeks ago, before sweeping his gaze around the room to identify potential bedmates and firing smouldering smiles at them scattergun.

'What?'

'You're right.'

'I am?'

As half a dozen women peeled themselves away from the throng and began to sidle over, Zander drained his glass and signalled for more drinks. 'Let's get this party started.'

CHAPTER TWO

By ONE-FIFTY IN the morning, Mia had sent Hattie and the team home in the van and returned to the kitchen.

Earlier in the evening she'd assumed that round about this time of night she'd be spending a few moments alone, communing with an empty and peaceful space and reflecting on a job well done. She'd imagined excitedly counting down the minutes until two and at that point going in search of Zander, telling him exactly what she wanted and heading off with him for a magical night of hot, steamy sex.

Now, however, while she was certainly watching the clock, she would not be tracking him down any time soon. She would not be telling him anything and the only place she'd be heading was home. Alone.

Too agitated to even think about reflecting on tonight's event with tranquillity and satisfaction, Mia paced the room and battled the urge to bang things together. Pans. Spoons. Her head against the wall.

She'd been such a fool, she inwardly railed as she ran out of space and spun on her heel to retrace her steps. And to think that not so long ago she'd been priding herself on her lack of stupidity. She was the absolute definition of it.

How could she ever have thought that sleeping with Zander would be a good idea?

She must have been out of her tiny little mind.

Because despite his coolly delivered observation when she'd handed him his dessert, the one that had upended her evening and made her feel somehow *special*, it had become blindingly obvious in the interim that she wasn't. Remotely. He didn't want *her*. He just wanted someone to take to bed tonight, someone to extend his birthday celebrations with, most probably. And evidently he didn't mind who.

Mia had nearly dropped the platter of truffles she'd been passing round when she'd caught him shooting come-hither smiles at certain female guests, a metaphorical crooking of his finger to which they'd instantly responded. What was going on? she'd wondered in a fluster of shock and confusion while just about managing to keep the professional smile pinned to her face. What had happened to two a.m.? Had he changed his mind? Was he playing some kind of game with her?

Well. She still had no answers to those questions, which had rocketed around her head for a good hour before she'd finally got a grip, but that was now fine because she was done with him. She was no one's toy. Zander could take his pick of the floozies he'd surrounded himself with, every single one of whom had spent the latter part of the evening vying for his attention, which he clearly hadn't minded *at all* because he'd hardly been fending them off. In fact, he could have the lot of them.

That his rejection stung was ridiculous. Hadn't she spent the last four months *not* wanting his attention? Yes, she'd changed her mind at the last minute, but she was clearly too late and what else had she expected? He was a man driven solely by carnality, so of course he'd move on. And now she thought about it, why *wouldn't* he have pursued her in the time they'd been planning this party? She was, after all, a female with a pulse. No wonder he'd kept throwing her suggestive looks and seductive smiles. His urge to flirt was instinctive. Innate. He simply couldn't help it.

But that was over. Once her invoice was settled, she need have nothing more to do with him. She would draw a line under everything and move on too. There was zero point wishing she'd accepted his invitation to dinner and slept with him when she'd had the chance and to hell with the consequences. Regret was a phenomenal waste of time. Tomorrow, work would return to normal, her own base desires would once again be back under her control, and she wouldn't miss any of it, not the flirting, not the attention, nothing.

The clock struck the hour, heralding the end of their contract. Filled with grim resolve, Mia stalked out of the kitchen, down a service corridor and across the deserted lobby. She pushed open the door to the cloakroom that was bigger than her entire flat and far more lavishly appointed and strode into the softly lit space, only to come to a dead stop at the sight of Zander shrugging on his jacket.

'What are you still doing here?' she said tetchily because he was still the sexiest man she'd ever seen and she still wanted him with every fibre of her being, and despite the extremely stern talking-to she'd just given herself, she *ached* with disappointment.

'I've just seen off the last of my guests,' he

said, his deep, gravelly tones irritatingly fluttering her stomach. 'How about you?'

'Finishing up in the kitchen.'

'Thank you for your services this evening.'

She flashed him a tight smile and headed for the one remaining item on the gleaming brass rails—her coat. 'No problem.'

'The food was excellent.'

'I'm pleased you enjoyed it.'

Blisteringly aware of his gaze tracking her every move, which was ironic when earlier he'd been so busy with his groupies he hadn't so much as *glanced* in her direction, Mia wrenched the garment off the hanger and pulled it on. She wrapped one side tight over the other and with a sharp yank tied the belt.

'Is something the matter?'

Annoyingly, she couldn't help snapping her gaze to him, even though she knew her cheeks were tellingly flushed and if looks could kill he'd likely be dead, which wasn't very professional, but professional was the last thing she was feeling right now. 'Why would anything be the matter?'

'I don't know,' he said coolly, reaching inside the sleeves of his jacket for the cuffs of his shirt and tugging them down. 'But you seem… upset.'

Upset was far too anodyne a word for the tangle of emotions that she was struggling to contain. 'I'm fine,' she said with another stiff smile. 'Just tired.'

'How are you getting home?'

At one stage this evening she'd thought she'd be going home with him. God, she was a fool. 'I'll catch a cab.'

'At this time on a Saturday night in central London?'

'I'm prepared to wait if I have to.'

'I'll take you.'

What? No? Absolutely not. Why prolong the agony? And anyway, surely he hadn't seen off *all* his guests. 'I'd have thought you'd have other…commitments.'

'What are you talking about?'

'Your…harem.'

His eyebrows shot up. 'My *what*?'

'All those women you summoned to your side,' she said crisply as she slipped her scarf off the hanger and looped it around her neck. 'The ones who then draped themselves over you, fawning and simpering, as if desperate to tend to your every need. I'm surprised you weren't sick after the number of truffles they fed you. But I must say, you did look very content with their company.'

'You sound jealous.'

She was. Hugely. And hurt. Which was absurd. 'Was that your intention?'

'No.'

'Well, I couldn't be less jealous,' she said with a casual shrug to prove it. 'It was just a bit nauseating to have to witness something like that in this day and age, that's all. You can sleep with whoever you choose. All of them at the same time if that's what floats your boat. It's none of my concern.'

'Then why do I get the feeling it is?'

'I have no idea. Why would I care what you do?'

'Beats me,' he drawled. 'You've made it very clear you're not interested in me, which I might not like but I do respect. I can see no reason at all why you would begrudge me seeking entertainment elsewhere.'

It was the thought of him doing exactly that, of showing some other woman the pleasure that should—and could—have been hers that made Mia snap. Without warning, the powerful mix of crushing disappointment, devastating hopelessness and the excoriating jealousy she'd just denied broke free, surging through her to steal her wits and her control.

'I'll tell you why,' she said hotly, her feet

propelling her across the thick pale grey carpet until she was a metre away from him, in his space, closer than she'd ever dared to get before. 'I begrudge it because you could not be more wrong about me not being interested in you. I've wanted you for *months*. Every time we've talked, every time we've messaged, whenever we've met up, all I've been able to think of is sex. With you. I've never been so attracted to anyone. I dream of your mouth. Of your hands on me and mine on you. I've taken more cold showers than I can count, not that they've worked.

'And before you tell me that I could have had you at any time,' she continued, unable to stop the roll she was on even if she'd wanted to, 'I couldn't. As you so astutely pointed out earlier this evening, I never let anything get in the way of business. There's just too much at stake for me. I want the financial security that success brings and I have every intention of getting it. So I've had to remain focused and keep you—my *client*—at arm's length. But that doesn't mean I haven't wanted to get up close and personal with you every minute of every day.'

She took a step towards him so he could not miss how very *upset* she was, even though his gaze was intent on her face already. 'You have no idea how hard it's been to resist you,' she said heatedly. 'How many times I've been on the verge of giving in. And then, when I was about to do exactly that, tonight, now, at two a.m., after *four months* of denial, which has been unbelievably tough to deal with, you decide to suddenly *abandon* the cat-and-mouse game you've been playing. You casually leave me high and dry and turn the spotlight elsewhere. It's just. Not. Fair.'

Finally running out of steam, Mia stopped, breathing hard, her head throbbing. Zander was staring down at her, utterly still. His eyes were dark and his jaw was rigid and his expression was so unreadable she didn't have a hope of working out what he might be thinking.

The silence thundered. The air between them crackled as if they'd whipped up their own little storm. For several long seconds neither of them moved.

But then, quite unexpectedly, he spun on his heel and stalked to the door, and she could have stamped her foot and screamed in frustration because was he really going to walk out? After everything she'd just confessed? What was wrong with him? With *her*?

But he didn't leave. He closed the door and

turned the key and the air whooshed from Mia's lungs. As he slowly wheeled round to retrace his steps, her heart gave a great crash against her ribs and then began to hammer.

He moved with the sleek languid stealth of a stalking panther. His heat-filled gaze locked onto hers like a laser and pinned her to the spot. Her mouth dried. The frustration and pique evaporated in a flash, and she realised with an electrifying thrill that ran the entire length of her body that he'd heard her. He'd taken on board everything she'd said and was shining his spotlight wholly on her and it was as glorious and exciting as she'd hoped.

'You want me to play fair?' he murmured thickly as he splayed his hands on her waist and backed her up against a wall, his voice so low and rough it vibrated in the marrow of her bones.

'I do,' she breathed, going willingly, giddily overwhelmed by his heat, his intoxicating scent, the sheer size and strength of him. 'I really do.'

The smile he gave her was faint but the heat in his gaze was fierce. His grip on her was light but she felt it like a brand. Need clawed at her stomach. Reason fled. He lowered his head and she closed her eyes and the last thing she heard before his mouth claimed hers in a kiss that short-circuited her brain was a soft, gruff, 'Then let's play.'

For someone with a supposedly super-agile brain, it had taken Zander a shockingly long time to reconcile his cool, efficient caterer with the smouldering siren whose passionate words had rendered him speechless and destroyed his reason. Then he'd had to process her astonishing confession and his immediate and dramatic response to it, which had made a complete mockery of both his belief that he'd finally put her from his mind and his assumption that any substitute would do, and that had taken some effort too.

Once he'd emerged from his stupor and recovered a grain of sanity, however, he'd briefly toyed with the option of telling her she was too late, but what on earth would be the point of that when he was so hard he hurt? Instead, he'd decided to punish her for putting him through such agony and riddling him with doubt these last few months, by slowly driving her to the brink of oblivion and keeping her there until she was panting and sobbing and begging him for mercy.

But it had been so long and he still wanted

her so much that the minute his mouth landed on hers the need for torture and revenge evaporated. All hope of steely control and cool finesse vanished. The kiss that Mia instantly returned with wild abandon ignited a fire in the pit of his stomach that shot flames along his veins, and when she moaned low in her throat and wrapped her arms tightly around his waist his restraint snapped.

Pressing her to the wall with his hips, Zander thrust his hands in her hair and angled her head to deepen the kiss. Desire pounded through him. Her scent addled what remained of his brain. How many times had he contemplated the plump softness of her lips? The smooth silk of her hair? The satiny texture of her skin? The reality easily surpassed anything he'd imagined.

When she pushed her hands beneath his shirt and planted them on his back, waves of heat radiated into every cell of his body. His muscles jumped and his skin sizzled, and though he'd thought he was as hard as he could be, she whimpered and writhed against him and proved him wrong.

Deeply relieved that he wasn't losing his touch, that she hadn't seen something in him that she didn't like but simply possessed an abundance of drive and ambition and a stubborn streak that rivalled his, needing to get closer, Zander broke off the kiss, breathing hard, and put just enough space between them to be able to untie the belt of her coat.

She looked charmingly dazed, he noted with satisfaction as he worked the knot free. Her blue eyes were glazed and her cheeks were flushed and she was breathing even more raggedly than he was. But then she blinked and put a staying hand on his and said urgently, 'Wait,' and he froze.

'What's wrong?' he rasped, thinking with his one remaining functioning brain cell that he might explode if they had to stop this now.

'Those women.'

He frowned. Reeled. Who? What the hell was she talking about? 'What women?'

'The moths to your flame.'

Ah. Right. Them. 'An attempt at distraction,' he muttered, rather regretting the move but at least understanding now why none of them had appealed. 'Which proved to be futile. So I sent them home. I've wanted you since the minute I laid eyes on you, Mia. Even after you turned down my invitation to dinner and drinks. You have no idea of the things I've imagined doing with you. You're not the only one who's been taking cold showers. Who's been going out of their mind. And, to add insult to injury, it would appear you've ruined me for anyone else.'

Her hands fell away from his, her head dropped back and a faint smile curved her gorgeous mouth. 'God, you're good,' she breathed as her gaze softened.

'I am,' he agreed, although, unusually, none of it was a line. He'd meant every word, which he did not want to analyse right now—or ever, for that matter, since navel-gazing was not his thing, unless literally. 'But know that you have no reason to be bothered by anyone.'

Clearly something in his tone or his expression reassured her because she said, 'We're wasting time,' and knocked his hands off her belt to take care of it herself.

His heart pounding, his need for her rushing back and hitting an almost unbearable high, Zander reached into his back pocket for his wallet. He shoved his trousers and shorts down and, with gritted teeth, rolled on protection. Mia slipped off her underwear and yanked up her dress and then, with hands that were strangely trembling, he gripped her thighs and lifted her up. She locked her legs around his waist and her arms around his neck and, unable to hold back a moment longer, he thrust into her warm, wet heat on a rough shuddery groan.

He cut off her cry with a kiss that was desperate and fierce and, powerless to wait, he began to move. He clasped her hips and she clutched at his hair and he tried to maintain control, but it had been four months and she felt like heaven. She was urging him on, panting and begging with increasing excitement, and he was fast unravelling.

Her legs tightened around his waist. Her inner muscles clenched around him as if she didn't want to ever let him go. Desperate for air, he wrenched his mouth from hers. As he slid it along her jaw, he could feel her ragged breath hot against his face. The exquisite tension in his muscles was building. His head was swimming and a wave of pleasure was beginning to ripple up from the base of his spine and he couldn't hold back any longer.

With a primitive growl, he nipped her earlobe and adjusted the angle of her hips and thrust hard, lodging so deep in her smooth, tight heat he saw stars. While she came apart, convulsing and trembling and pressing her mouth to his neck to muffle her cry, he shattered, pulsating into her relentlessly and burying his face in the crook of her neck as white-hot ecstasy crashed through him.

How long they stayed there locked together, hearts pounding against each other, slowing as they began to recover, he couldn't have said. It was only once the adrenalin had drained from his body, turning his muscles to mush and rendering his legs so weak they could barely hold him up, that he lifted his head from her neck, gently eased from her and set her down.

'So that was good,' Mia murmured hoarsely, blinking as if stunned, still plastered to the wall as if moving away from it might land her in a boneless heap on the floor.

Zander turned away to deal with the condom and thought that good was an understatement. Never before had lights actually flashed behind his eyelids. Never before had undoing one gorgeous yet stubborn woman given him such satisfaction.

'You really do live up to your reputation.'

'I've barely even started,' he muttered, briefly wondering whether the fact that he'd never surrendered control to such mindlessness before either was a concern or merely the consequence of four months of abstinence. 'We have months to make up for and I have plans for your scarf.'

'Well, we can't stay here,' she observed with breathless excitement and a glance at the door that wouldn't remain locked for ever.

She was right. They couldn't. So, the only question that remained was, 'Your place or mine?'

CHAPTER THREE

Seven weeks later

'STILL NO REPLY?'

With a scowl, Mia shoved her frustratingly silent phone into the back pocket of her jeans and reached for a giant colander. 'Nothing,' she said, dumping it in the sink and heading to the fridge.

Hattie, who was blitzing a pile of parsley and thyme with a gleaming ten-inch knife, grimaced. 'What's the tally now?'

'Twelve calls, fifteen messages and seven emails in total.'

'Maybe he's somewhere that doesn't have a mobile signal or Wi-Fi.'

'For forty-eight hours?'

'Yeah, I guess that is pretty unlikely,' came the dry response. 'Your emails now go straight into his junk mail folder, then. He's deleted you from his contacts and doesn't answer calls from unknown numbers.'

Retrieving the mussels—the main course for tonight's dinner party for twenty—Mia had to admit that that explanation for Zander's lack of response to her attempts at communication wasn't beyond the realms of possibility. The morning after the incredible night they'd spent incinerating her sheets, when she'd woken up to find him gone, no note, no nothing, she'd neatly excised him from her life too, although luckily, given recent developments, she did at least archive past clients' correspondence details.

'Even so,' she said, slicing open the netted bag and pouring its contents into the colander, 'you'd think that a text saying, I'M PREGNANT, CALL ME!—in caps—might have generated *some* sort of response. I mean, as messages go, it's not exactly ambiguous.'

'Perhaps he really is as heartless as his reputation suggests.'

Physically he wasn't, of course. Many times that night Mia had felt it thundering beneath her palm as they hurtled again and again into blissful oblivion.

His morning-after etiquette, however, left a lot to be desired, she reflected as she switched on the tap and swirled the colander around beneath it.

Not that she was still smarting over the way he'd disappeared or anything. Well aware of his reputation, she hadn't expected him to linger over breakfast and then suggest a romantic walk in the park. A 'thanks for a fun time' and a goodbye might have been nice, but she'd never had a one-night stand before—it had never struck her as the best way of achieving the commitment she was after—so who knew? Presumably, rendering women boneless with pleasure and then sneakily creeping from their bed while they recovered was his modus operandi.

'I accept that he may have forgotten me,' she said, wincing at the unflattering thought, made worse by the fact that, despite her every effort, she had not forgotten him. 'But even a "who is this?" would be better than complete radio silence.'

'Could he have blocked you?'

'How would I know?'

'Try my phone.'

Mia put down the mussels and switched off the tap, then took the device Hattie was holding out. She entered the number that was now etched into her memory, hit the button to dial it and braced herself for the impact of Zander's deep, spine-tingling voice pouring into her ear. But, as she'd expected, it rang a couple of times and went to an automated voicemail, and there didn't seem much point in leaving yet another message.

'This doesn't work either,' she said, handing the phone back with a tut of irritation.

'So what will you do next?'

It was an excellent question, and right now Mia was all out of answers. She was weak from having thrown up for seven mornings in a row. She was still in shock from discovering two days ago that she was pregnant and not, as she'd initially wondered, suffering from either a bug or food poisoning. Hattie, to whom she'd had to confess almost everything after gagging violently at the sight of some undressed squid, was doing her best to be helpful, but her failure to contact the father of her baby was only adding to her stress, and she was exhausted.

'Quite honestly, I'd like to go and lie down in a dark room and stay there for a month,' she said, heaving the colander out of the sink and setting it on the side.

'You can't,' said Hattie, aghast.

'I know.'

However tempting, running away and hiding wasn't an option. Not only did she not do that any more, but also Christmas was Halliday Catering's busiest time of the year. Bookings were pretty much back to back for the next five weeks, and she would not let anyone down.

Nor would she give up on Zander until she'd turned over every stone in her efforts to speak to him. He had the right to know she was pregnant with his child. How involved he wanted to be, if at all, was his choice to make and she would not deprive him of that.

She'd never known her own father. She too was the product of a one-night stand, the irony of which did not escape her. But at least she knew the father of *her* baby's name. Her mother had not. In fact, her mother had known very little about the stranger she'd met in a nightclub thirty-one years ago, which had made tracking him down to inform him of his impending fatherhood impossible.

Growing up, Mia had felt his absence keenly. No amount of daydreaming about who and where he might be and what he might be doing had filled the yawning gap inside her. Reason and fortitude had been no match for the rejection and the longing she'd experienced.

If her father had been around when her mother had fallen ill with dementia, she might have had an easier time of it. She might have felt less shamefully resentful and angry at the

situation that was no one's fault. As she'd ma-
tured, she'd come to terms with living with
the empty space that her father should have
occupied but she would never willingly or deliberately foist that aching sense of loss and
abandonment on any child of hers.

And then there was the paralysing fear that
if something happened to her, her child would
be left on its own, with no one to care for them
and no one to rely on. Tests had shown that she
didn't carry the gene that had caused her mother's illness, so her risk of young-onset dementia
was no greater than anyone else's, but plenty
of other things could befall her. She could be
run over by a bus or get sick with some other
disease, and in the event of her untimely de-
mise there was no one else. Apart from Zander.

'So?'

Pulling herself together and returning to the
present, Mia snapped on a pair of latex gloves.
'I'm going to have to carry on looking for him
until I find him.'

'How are you going to do that?'

Wasn't that the million-dollar question? 'I
have absolutely no idea.'

Alone in the boardroom after a three-hour
meeting to which he'd paid unusually scant at-

tention, Zander surged to his feet and snatched his coat off a peg. The glass walls were closing in on him. His chest was tight and his head pounded. He needed to move. He needed some air.

The restlessness that had set in over the last month was getting worse, he thought grimly as he strode to the lift and jabbed at the button. The niggling sense of dissatisfaction and the strange ennui, which he just couldn't seem to shake, no matter how busy he kept himself both professionally and socially, were becoming increasingly intolerable.

Maybe he was burning out.

Or perhaps turning thirty-five had triggered a mid-life crisis.

The lift arrived and in he stepped.

Could he be getting old?

No. He was in his prime. At the height of success with a lifestyle that he knew many envied.

The flurry of invitations to weddings and christenings he'd received recently suggested that the people around him were moving on, but he was fine exactly where he was. He wanted a wife and kids like a hole in the head. Even if he *had* possessed the necessary skill set to maintain a relationship, which he did not, why anyone would willingly put their emotions out there to be dismissed at best and destroyed at worst was completely beyond him.

Only once had he made the mistake of letting someone get too close. He'd met Valentina at a party on Zakynthos at the age of nineteen, and had instantly been dazzled. They'd dated for six months, during which he'd tried to give her what she wanted and to form the kind of attachment others seemed to have no trouble achieving, even introducing her to his siblings. But ultimately he'd failed because, as she'd told him when she'd been breaking up with him, he was emotionally void, in possession of a heart of stone and incapable of giving anything of himself to anyone, other than his body.

That experience had left him feeling wounded and bewildered. It had dredged up memories of his youth and stirred feelings of inadequacy that he'd believed he'd conquered long before. Determined to never have to go through anything like that again, hating the weakness and pain it had caused, he'd vowed to remain alone and untouchable, strong and safe. And by keeping his emotions buried and his defences up, he had. Successfully. For years.

So meaningless one-night stands that

scratched an itch but never probed any deeper? Great. Love and commitment? Very much not.

Most probably it was the time of year that was making him feel so unsettled, he figured, shrugging on his coat as the lift began its smooth, silent descent. He'd never liked Christmas with its emphasis on festivity and family. He couldn't remember a time the members of his had celebrated it all together. His mother had always jetted off in early December in search of winter sun and unencumbered fun, and still did. His father, before his fatal heart attack eighteen years ago, had believed that children should be seen and not heard and had therefore spent as little time as possible in their company—with the exception of Leo, the heir to the family business—even on Christmas Day. Zander had invariably spent the holidays kicking around the mansion in Athens with the five siblings he increasingly failed to understand and the two nannies, stuffing his face with *kourabiedes* and wondering where the jollity was.

The lift came to a sibilant stop at the ground floor, putting the brakes on his turbulent thoughts not a moment too soon. The doors opened and he was immediately hit by the not unpleasant scent of a wintry forest, courtesy of the thirty-metre Nordic spruce being craned into place in the centre of the lobby, and a faintly desperate female voice coming from the reception area which stopped him in his tracks and froze him to the spot.

'He *has* to be here. I read there was a board meeting today. Where else would he be?'

His pulse leapt. His breath caught. He recognised that voice. The last time he'd heard it, it had been panting in his ear, begging him to go harder, faster, deeper. He recognised the red-gold hair too, rippling out from beneath a navy bobble hat. He could still recall the silky feel of it tangled around his fingers and sweeping over his skin.

Mia.

A woman who irritatingly refused to remain in the past and continued to haunt his dreams.

What was she doing here?

Why was she looking for him?

Catching his eye, the receptionist gave a subtle nod in the direction of the security guard and raised her eyebrows in silent question. Zander shook his head because avoidance might have been his parents' style but it certainly wasn't his, and already Mia was attracting attention.

He strode across the white marble floor towards the woman who'd turned out to be infinitely more disturbing than he'd ever envisaged. In response to the receptionist's gesture, she spun on her heel and, as her gaze collided with his, it occurred to him belatedly that he should have spent those few frozen moments bracing himself for her impact. While he vividly recalled every detail of what they'd once done to each other, he'd forgotten how breathtaking she was in the flesh.

'Aha!' she said, flashing him a dazzling smile that struck him like a blow to the gut. 'Finally! You're a hard man to track down, Zander Stanhope. Did you block my number?'

He had. He'd had to. The night they'd spent together had rocked his world. So much so that he'd forced himself to leave before she woke up and tempted him to stay for a week, a month, for ever.

Not that that had put an end to his bizarre fixation with her. He'd lost count of the times he'd considered calling her up and inviting her over for more. On one particularly alarming occasion his finger had hovered over her name for several seconds before a warning signal had sounded in his brain, reminding him of his once-only policy, and snapped him out of it. Deleting her details hadn't been enough.

He couldn't risk her contacting him, weakening, and all those buried emotions and bizarre doubts stirring again. He'd had to go nuclear.

'It was nothing personal,' he said, directing her behind a wall of greenery that would afford them a small degree of privacy.

'So *you* think.'

'I apologise.'

'I don't believe you mean that,' she said with disconcerting perception. 'Do you get personal with any of the women you sleep with?'

'No.' Not these days.

'Too many of them to bother with?'

Quite the opposite. In fact, he hadn't taken anyone to bed since Mia. Over a month ago. Which, come to think of it, perhaps explained his restlessness. 'Something like that.'

'So you block them,' she said with a rueful shake of her beautiful head. 'Harsh. Nevertheless, I wish you'd kept me in your phone. I've been trying to contact you since Thursday. I've sent you countless emails and texts and left numerous voicemails. You haven't made it easy.'

That had been the plan.

But why had she wanted to contact him? And why since Thursday? Had she been as affected by what they'd done as he had? Could she not stand the frustration any longer? He ignored the quick surge of his pulse at the thought of it and refocused.

'I'll admit the night we spent together was good,' he said, blocking the hot, distracting memories that were trying to barge their way into his head. 'Very good, in fact.' The best he'd ever had, even. 'But it was still just one night.'

'Well, that was certainly the *intention*.'

'What do you mean?'

'We need to talk.'

On the contrary, they did not need to talk. He'd already spent far too long on this unexpected conversation, and he didn't appreciate the effect she was having on him, even after all this time. He should never have indulged his curiosity in the first place by talking to her. What on earth had he been thinking?

'No, we don't,' he said, beginning to regret that he hadn't left her to Security after all.

'It won't take long,' she said, with irritating disregard for his objection. 'Can we go somewhere a bit more private?'

Absolutely not. He didn't want to be alone with her when she put him so on edge. He didn't want to be anywhere with her full stop, and if he had to be brutal to reinforce that point, then so be it.

'I'm not after a relationship, Mia,' he said,

his voice low so as not to be overheard through the bamboo. 'I never have been. I thought that was clear.'

'It was,' she replied, leaning towards him, equally discreet. 'It was crystal clear. And neither am I. At least, not with you. That's *not* why I'm here.'

Good. That was a relief. So why was he suddenly wondering, why not him? What was wrong with *him*? It was an absurd and unnecessary thought—he knew exactly what was wrong with him—so he shoved it aside and focused.

'Then why *are* you here?' he said, ignoring her dizzying proximity and the scent he apparently hadn't forgotten. 'Is there a problem with the payment of your invoice?'

'No.'

'Do you have some other business involving my company?'

'No.'

'Are you in trouble?'

'Not exactly.'

'I don't have time for riddles,' he said, his surging frustration at the way she was addling his brain *finally* igniting some strength of character. 'And I fail to see anything else we might have to discuss, so if you'll excuse me, I have somewhere else to be.'

Wrenching himself away from her compelling gaze before he drowned in it, Zander turned on his heel, intending to round the screen and head for the exit, practically tasting fresh air and freedom, only to come to an abrupt stop when she spoke, the words flying through the space and landing on him like darts.

'I'm pregnant.'

CHAPTER FOUR

AT MIA'S ANNOUNCEMENT, every cell of Zander's body froze. His head emptied and he went numb. Beyond the bamboo, people moved. Outside on the street, traffic flowed. The world continued turning, even if here, behind the plants, it had shuddered to a halt.

Slowly, warily, his pulse thudding so loudly he could hear it in his ears, he turned back to face her. 'What did you say?'

'I'm pregnant,' she repeated, chin up, shoulders squared as if ready for battle. 'And the baby's yours.'

He gave his head one sharp shake of denial. That couldn't be right. 'No.'

'Yes, as a matter of fact. I did a test a week ago. Well, four, actually. Just in case. All were positive and it was later confirmed by my doctor. You're the father, Zander. You're the only person I've slept with in two years.'

White noise. That was all he could hear beyond her words. A loud rushing nothingness that obliterated everything in its path. 'How is that possible?'

She flushed. 'I've been focusing on my career,' she said defensively. 'And not everyone has a different person in their bed each week.'

Her barb bounced straight off him. As if his sex life, or lack of it, was of any significance right now. 'I was talking about protection,' he said, struggling to claw back some of the trademark languor that was rapidly deserting him. 'Which we used.'

'No contraception is one hundred percent foolproof,' she said, wrapping her coat around herself more tightly, as if warding off a chill. 'And we put it to the test a lot.'

They had. Once they'd got to her flat, they'd tested it on the console table in her hall. Her shower, her sofa and her bed, over and over again.

So much heat…

So much pleasure…

So irrelevant right now.

'It's a shock,' she said, her voice muffled by the shrieking chaos swirling around inside him. 'I get that. It was to me too when I found out. I thought I had food poisoning or a bug or something. Even when I'd worked out the dates, I didn't want to believe it. It still doesn't seem real, to be honest. I don't expect anything from you, Zander. I just thought you should know, that's all. If you want to be involved in this child's life, that would be great. I never knew my own father and I wish I had. So I'd like us to do this together, however that works. I'm aware it wouldn't be easy. Our lives are very different. There'd be compromises and sacrifices, which I'm willing to make.'

She paused, presumably to give him the opportunity to respond, but he had nothing. Absolutely nothing. He was sinking into quicksand, already up to his neck, and there was no rope to hand to pull himself free.

'However, if none of that appeals,' she continued after a moment, 'then fine. It's my choice to have this baby. The circumstances aren't ideal, I admit, but I've always wanted children. I'm thirty and single and this might be my only chance. However, I'm perfectly capable of doing it on my own. I believe that having you around would be best for our child, but I don't *need* you. You're under no obligation from me to do anything. You could walk away right now, and that would be fine. Whatever you decide, Zander, it's entirely up to you.'

It was unfortunate that the degree of his involvement in this was entirely up to him because right now he was utterly incapable of making a decision. He could barely think straight. He felt light-headed. He couldn't breathe. His chest was tingling and his stomach was churning and all the blood in his body was rushing to his feet.

He needed a minute. He needed a drink. But the nearest bottle of industrial strength liquor was in his office, which was far too far away, so he had to make do with focusing on his breathing, in and out, deep and slow, until the threat of keeling over receded.

Theos.

How the hell could this have happened? He'd always been so careful. He didn't want a kid. He never had. He wasn't equipped to be a father. He'd be useless. He couldn't even keep a houseplant alive. What hope would he have of successfully raising an actual human being?

It wasn't as if he'd had a good role model. His own father had been cold and distant, so intolerant of tears and emotion of any kind that Zander had swiftly learned to suppress both. Support, interest, praise, affection—he'd had none of that, although there'd been plenty of criticism and discipline. His mother had been no better. Every time she'd looked at him, it was as if she were surprised to see him there, as if she'd forgotten he existed.

He knew nothing of emotional connection and communication, so what if *his* son or daughter needed something from him that he was simply unable to provide? Would the patterns of the past repeat themselves? Might no father be better than a bad one? Wouldn't Mia ably fill both roles? Shouldn't he take the escape route she'd given him, declare he wanted to have nothing do with them and leave them both better off?

On the other hand, Leo, his older brother, seemed to be doing all right with *his* family. As the heir to the Stanhope Kallis empire, he'd received the lion's share of their father's attention growing up, but it hadn't been warm, and their mother had been just as negligent with him. However, Leo was soppy as hell over his two daughters and madly in love with his wife.

What if he—Zander—decided he couldn't turn his back on his child and subject him or her to the neglect and rejection he'd experienced as a youth and, against all the odds, the same thing happened to him? Not the loving a wife part—no one would ever get close enough for that because, if they did, the gaping lack of a soul they'd find would send them running for the hills—but the sentimentality over a child.

What if he decided to try and do better than his pathetic excuse for parents, learning from those of his siblings with offspring, perhaps, became invested in the pregnancy and the baby and then did something to mess it all up? If, in the course of their co-parenting, Mia decided he just wasn't good enough—after all, as she'd pointed out, she didn't *need* him—she could cut him out completely, and where would that leave him then?

No. He would not allow that to happen. Such vulnerability was unacceptable. He couldn't abandon this child of his—that wasn't the man he was or wanted to be—and he could hardly do a worse job than either of his parents had. Therefore, he had to secure his position. Lock this thing down on his terms. As he did day in, day out, at work. So that when he did screw things up, as he undoubtedly would, Mia couldn't just take off with their child, leaving him broken, alone, with nothing for company but emptiness.

Quashing the doubts and thinking purely of his position, Zander set his jaw. He pulled himself up to his full height, looked directly at the woman who'd just tossed a grenade into his life and altered it for good, and said, 'We'd better get married.'

Blurting out her news in the middle of the busy lunchtime lobby, even from behind a dense wall of foliage, had not been Mia's intention when she'd decided to ambush Zander at his office. However, he hadn't given her a choice. She'd spent *days* trying to get hold of him—she'd even contemplated hiring a private investigator if today's efforts had proven fruitless—and it had been beyond stressful, so she had not been about to let him push her aside and stalk off without knowing the truth.

Understandably, he'd been stunned by her news. He'd inhaled as if winded and gone so white she'd feared he was about to faint. Once she'd finished explaining, she'd wondered whether she could have rendered him permanently speechless. But then he'd responded, with a proposal no less, and now it was her turn to be shocked.

What planet was he on? Marriage for the sake of a baby? In *this* day and age? Even she, with all her concerns about what might or might not happen in the future, didn't think that necessary. Besides, he was the ultimate no-strings-attached wonder. Why on earth would he even *want* to get married?

'I don't think there's any need to be quite so dramatic,' she said, once she'd unglued her tongue from the roof of her mouth.

'I would like to guarantee my rights.'

Her heart gave a little leap of hope. 'So you want to be involved?'

He nodded. 'At every stage.'

Oh, thank God for that. 'Well, that's good,' she said with what had to be the understatement of the century when he'd just allayed her greatest fear by indicating that if something happened to her he'd step up. 'But marriage is unnecessary. I would never prevent you from being part of anything. I grew up without knowing my father and I would never deliberately do that to my child. You have my word.'

'I don't know if I can count on your word,' he said curtly. 'Not on this.'

Ouch. 'You can count on the law.'

'That's not enough.'

Zander folded his arms across his broad, solid chest, which she'd once explored at length, his expression implacable, his dark gaze steely, and it occurred to her suddenly that the delicious wickedness she'd always associated with him was no longer there. In fact, she could see no hint of the playboy she'd become acquainted with while planning his party. Or the towering inferno she'd taken to bed. In front of her, pinning her to the spot from a deliberate position of dominance, was an altogether more dangerous sort of man, a man with a reputation for ruthlessness as well as seduction, who got what he wanted, whatever the cost, a force to be reckoned with.

But she would not be intimidated. Or distracted, no matter how unexpectedly thrilling she found this particular version of him. Thanks to her tough adolescence, she was no pushover either and she certainly wasn't going to agree to something neither of them had had time to consider. Plenty of people had children out of wedlock. It was hardly taboo these days.

And anyway, when she got married it would be for love. She wanted a husband who adored her, and a genuine partnership based on friendship and respect. She hadn't just dreamed of creating a successful business and gaining financial security all these years. She also, perhaps even more desperately, yearned for a family. She'd been on her own for so long, and in the quiet early hours of the morning, when she hadn't been able to sleep and sometimes still couldn't, she ached with loneliness that grew by the day.

Admittedly, she hadn't had much luck on that front. When it came to relationships, she knew she came across as clingy and needy, pushing for too much too soon, because she'd been told so by her last boyfriend while he'd been breaking up with her. And in the aftermath, during which she'd forced herself to revisit and analyse her two relationships before that one, she'd discovered a pattern that, with hindsight, was pretty self-destructive.

She'd vowed to do things differently next time, to remove the pressure and let things play out at their own speed, but 'differently' did not mean blindly tying herself to a man she barely knew simply because she was pregnant and he didn't trust her.

'Well, it'll have to be enough for now,' she said firmly, refusing to indulge his posturing and needing to escape both the unsettling intensity with which he was looking at her and the bizarre desire to step in closer. 'It's far too early to be talking about that sort of commitment. Or any sort of commitment, for that matter. The first trimester can be precarious and, according to the doctor, I'm only a couple of months into it. Anything could happen in the next few weeks. So let's just see how things go.'

As CEO of one of the world's largest privately owned companies, 'seeing how things went' was not Zander's preferred way of doing things and if Mia hadn't shot off before he'd had the time and the head space to process the stunning realisation that she'd challenged him, he'd have informed her of that fact.

But in the days that followed he repeatedly revisited their conversation and eventually concluded that in this situation the unilateral decision-making and expecting everyone to go along with it that he was used to was probably not going to work. Mia wasn't one of his employees or a potential business partner. She was the mother of his child, with opinions of her own.

However, he wasn't unduly worried. There was plenty of time to persuade her to see things his way. Everyone did, in the end, and he remained ever more convinced that marriage was the only way to guarantee the outcome he desired. His request for her birth certificate so he could begin the paperwork had so far gone unanswered, but if that situation persisted he'd simply request a copy of the public document for himself.

He had plenty of time too to get a grip on the idea of impending fatherhood. Having unblocked Mia's number and reinstated her as a contact, he'd read her messages and listened to her voicemails, and the news was sinking in. Gradually.

At some point he'd find a way through the chaos in his head, he was certain. He wouldn't be riding this weird, frustratingly irrepressible roller coaster of panic and confusion, pride and elation for ever and he'd soon tire of imagining what the kid he'd created with Mia might look like.

Unwelcome thoughts of his own parents and his relationship with them kept popping up to plague him, which was annoying when that bore no relevance to anything, but with effort he was just about managing to suppress at least those. His entire life had been turned upside down. It was only natural for his thoughts to be in disarray and his focus to be off.

'Are you listening to a word I've been saying?'

From behind his desk, Zander stifled a sigh and returned his attention to his one surviving parent, his mother, who'd waltzed into his officc ten minutes ago without an appointment, swathed in caramel cashmere and indignation. 'Your dividends are down this year because we've invested heavily in the Kallis side of the business,' he said. 'We bought a fleet of cruise ships and overhauled six of the shipyards. It was all in the shareholders' report. Did you read it?'

Selene pouted. 'No.'

There was a surprise. 'Your income will be back to seven figures next year.'

'What am I meant to do in the meantime?'

With the several hundreds of thousands of euros she'd still receive? Quite honestly, he didn't care. 'You could try economising.'

'I don't even know what that means,' she said petulantly. 'You're more of a disappointment than Leo was when he sat behind that desk. I never thought *you* would spoil my fun too. I do miss your father.'

Selene's criticism ricocheted off his armour without making so much as a dent, but miss his father? That was a joke. Not only had the ink barely had time to dry on the marriage certificate before she'd embarked on a string of affairs that she'd made little attempt to hide, but also the only person she had any sort of feeling for was herself. Edward Stanhope had been so busy merging his banking empire with Selene's shipping one, which he'd acquired on their marriage, he'd turned a blind eye to his wife's scandalous behaviour and her profligacy, and it was that that she missed.

'You'll survive.'

'I don't know how. You'll be tossing me out of the house and onto the streets next.'

Zander gritted his teeth and resisted the urge to tell his mother to grow up because that approach had never worked. 'Was there anything else?' he asked instead. Such as, say, an enquiry into how he was. What plans he might have for Christmas. Whether he had any major news to impart.

'No,' she said, rising elegantly from the chair and throwing one end of her scarf over her shoulder. 'I'm late for my flight as it is, and I don't suppose they'll hold it for me. Really, this is a very inconvenient time of year for the jet to have a technical fault. It's eleven hours to the Maldives. It's going to be ghastly, even in first class.'

From habit, Zander got up too, and was about to stride to the door to open it to let his mother and her eternal disappointment in him out when his phone rang. He glanced down at the screen and, on seeing who it was, stopped in his tracks.

'Excuse me,' he muttered with a frown. 'I need to take this. You can see yourself out.'

With a huff and a pointed comment about manners, his mother flounced from his office, but all Zander was interested in now was why Mia was calling him after four days' silence. Could she have considered his proposal and concluded it was for the best? Was that why his pulse had spiked? Because he'd won?

'Mia.'

'Hi,' she said. 'Are you busy?'

Always. He had a series of meetings this Monday afternoon and the delightful interlude with his mother had already set him back half an hour. But something in her voice concerned him. He thought he could detect a note of desperation behind her words and a certain raggedness to her breathing, and he didn't like any of it.

'No,' he said. 'I'm not. What's going on?'

'I'm bleeding, Zander, and I'm cramping. It hurts. A lot. I think I may be miscarrying.'

His blood froze. His heart stopped. The ground rocked beneath his feet and his stomach went into freefall, which meant that he had to ignore the sudden crushing pressure in his chest and switch to the practical. 'Where are you?'

'On my way to hospital,' she said with a sharp intake of breath that turned into a shuddery sort of a sob.

'Text me the details,' he said, already at the lift that would zoom him down to the garage, with his coat, his wallet, his keys. 'I'll be there as soon as I can.'

CHAPTER FIVE

MIA EMERGED FROM the clinic a lot less terrified than she'd been when she'd gone in. She'd never felt fear like it and hoped never to again.

It had all happened so suddenly. One minute she'd been deboning a chicken while humming along to the radio, in an effort to not think about Zander's arrogant presumption in emailing his request for her birth certificate, as if her feelings on the subject of marriage were so immaterial they could simply be bulldozed to bits, the next a shooting pain had sliced across her abdomen and a wet warmth had seeped between her legs.

Stunned, devastated, she'd dropped the knife and doubled over, clutching at her midriff, tears springing to her eyes, a voice in her head screaming *No, no, no!*

With trembling hands, her chest aching as if her heart had been yanked out, she'd called her doctor, who'd advised her to go straight to hospital, and then she'd rung Zander. She had no idea why. It wasn't as if she didn't have friends and, for all she knew, her number might still be blocked. But it wasn't. He must have meant what he'd said about intending to be involved at every stage and reinstated it.

When he'd turned up at the hospital ten minutes after her, however, taking charge and demanding answers, she'd never been so glad to see anyone in her life. She really hadn't wanted to go through whatever she was going through alone, and why *wouldn't* she have called him when anything to do with the pregnancy and their baby was his business too? He'd dealt with the estimated eight-hour wait by whisking her off to a private clinic where she'd been seen immediately, and she was now even more convinced she'd made the right decision in contacting him.

Still shaky and raw, despite the positive outcome of the appointment, Mia pushed through the door that opened into the lobby, her gaze landing on the man pacing up and down in front of the reception desk. In his beautiful charcoal grey coat that probably cost more than she turned over in a month, he looked far more at home here among the wood panelling and cream carpet than the chaos of Accident and Emergency.

'Well?' he said, striding over to her, his jaw tight as he raked his gaze over her.

'Everything's fine.'

He came to an abrupt stop and his brows snapped together. Shadows lurked in the depths of his eyes and his thick dark hair was dishevelled. 'Fine?' he demanded. 'What do you mean, fine? You look as if you've been crying.'

That was because she had. But not with grief. 'The baby's OK,' she hastened to assure him with a stab at a watery smile. 'We're both OK.'

'Are you certain?'

'So I've been told.'

'You're not miscarrying?'

'No. I had an ultrasound. I heard the heartbeat. It sounded a bit like galloping horses. It was kind of mind-blowing.'

And the relief when the quick, strong, rhythmic pulses had filled the room... God, the *relief*. She'd wept with it and only just refrained from hugging the sonographer when he'd told her everything was all right.

'They gave me two pictures of the baby,' she said, swallowing down the hot, tight lump in her throat and blinking back the fresh sting of tears. 'Here. This one's for you.'

As she handed him the tiny black and white photo his fingers touched hers and an unexpected sizzle of heat rushed through her. He stared at the grainy image, thankfully too absorbed in it to notice the tiny gasp she gave in both shock and horror, because here and now was neither the time nor the place for that sort of thing, and muttered something in Greek before falling silent.

Determinedly ignoring the memories of the steamy night they'd spent together, which were now inappropriately trying to muscle their way in to her head, Mia sought to fill the oddly intimate quiet.

'I feel a bit foolish, actually,' she said, shifting her weight from one foot to the other, her cheeks heating when she recalled how overwrought she'd been when she'd called him. 'There was pain and blood, and I automatically assumed the worst. But apparently it's not that uncommon at this stage of pregnancy. I'm so sorry to have dragged you away from work for nothing.'

'Forget it.'

That was unlikely. She didn't think she'd *ever* forget the terror and the desolation she'd felt. 'Thank you for your help.'

'Any time,' he muttered as he tucked the

photo into the top inside pocket of his coat. 'So is that it?' He lifted his dark gaze to hers, his expression oddly inscrutable. 'No treatment? You don't need to stay here for observation?'

'No, that's it,' she said. 'Well, I was advised to rest for a week or two,' she amended with a faint frown, 'but that's not likely to happen. I mean it's December and I'm a caterer. It's my busiest time of year. Tonight, for example, I have a drinks party for a hundred.'

His eyebrows shot up. 'A hundred?'

'Yes.'

'Tonight?'

'Yes.'

'Cancel it. In fact, cancel everything.'

She blinked up at him in shock. 'What? No. I can't possibly do that. It'll destroy my business.'

There was a second of stunned silence before he spoke. 'Are you *serious*?'

'It's all right for you and your three-hundred-year-old billion-euro company,' she said, bristling in response to his incredulous arrogance. 'Mine is at a crucial stage, both reputationally and financially. I can't just cancel events that have been months in the planning. I promise I'll take it easy. I'll make sure I sit down when I can and drink lots of water.'

'And risk this happening again? Only for real?'

That sobered her up. The dizzying relief and the adrenalin rushing through her system evaporated in an instant and her chest tightened as a cold sweat broke out all over her skin.

Because Zander had a point.

How could she possibly continue as planned, as if this afternoon had been nothing more than a minor inconvenience? Even though she'd been assured there was no reason to suspect it *would* happen again, every minute of every day and night she'd be worried. And rightly so, because she'd even told him that the first three months could be precarious.

This pregnancy wasn't some sort of abstract idea, as it had felt up until now. The baby growing inside her had a shape and a heartbeat and already she loved it fiercely. Currently, it was dependent entirely on her for its well-being, so she had to stop thinking solely of herself. Even Zander wasn't doing that. By putting the baby first, not only was he proving that he'd fully step in if something happened to her, thank God, but also he was behaving in the way she supposed most fathers-to-be would, although what would she know when she hadn't had one of her own?

In fact, her child was enviably lucky to have two present and engaged parents. She wanted to make that work, so perhaps now was the time for one of the sacrifices she'd told him in the lobby of his building that she'd be willing to make.

'You're right,' she conceded, swiftly working through the practicable options while trying and failing to process both the enormous reality of her situation and her complicated feelings about fathers. 'Of course you're right.'

'Stanhope Kallis has a corporate entertainment department,' said Zander, a fraction calmer than a moment ago although, judging by the set of his jaw, no less determined to get his way. 'I can parachute in a substitute events organiser right now.'

'That won't be necessary.'

'Why not?'

'Because *I* have someone who can temporarily take over,' she said without hesitation, while nevertheless inwardly wincing at the thought of giving up control of the company to which she'd dedicated the last six years of her life, however briefly. 'Hattie. Harriet. My number two. She's been with me since the beginning and I trust her implicitly. All the menus for December have been finalised and the food is on order. It's just a question of logistics now and she's more than capable of handling those. I can get in more staff to help her, if needs be, and I'll be on the end of the phone.'

After a moment's consideration, he gave a short nod. 'That would be acceptable.'

Was it now. 'I'm delighted you think so,' she said dryly.

Planting a hand on her lower back, which bizarrely she could feel, despite the thick layers of clothing she was wearing, Zander steered her with care in the direction of the exit.

What was she going to *do* for a fortnight? she wondered as she tried to ignore both his disconcerting proximity and the touch that felt almost protective. She hadn't had so much time off in years. Maybe she could work on some new recipes. Or tweak her five-year forecast. She could even put up those shelves that had been propped up against the living room wall for months.

And when the inevitable boredom set in?

Well, surely an *occasional* trip to the unit to see how things were going wouldn't hurt. She would, of course, leave any heavy lifting to others, but she could easily peel a potato. Rinsing a lettuce or whipping up a quick *beurre blanc* didn't exactly require much in the way of effort.

And if she found herself just happening to pass by a venue at which an event she'd organised was taking place, it would be only natural to drop in for a moment. The client would be expecting it. In fact, wouldn't it actually be *good* for her and the baby if she checked in from time to time? Wouldn't the stress of worrying about how her business was faring in her absence be worse?

'One more thing,' Zander said as he released her to reach for the door.

'What?'

'You're moving in with me.'

Mia froze in the process of pulling on her gloves and shot him a startled glance. What? No. How would she be able to keep an eye on things if he was keeping an eye on her? And did she really want him witnessing the unpleasantness of morning sickness, even if it did seem to be easing? She did not.

'Oh, there's no need for that,' she said with an airy wave and a reassuring smile. 'I have a perfectly good flat of my own. It has central heating and running water and everything. You should know. You've been there.'

For a split second she thought she saw a flicker of heat light the dark depths of his eyes, as if he were remembering not only being there but everything they'd done within its four walls. But a moment later it was gone and he was pulling open the door and standing to one side and she figured she must have been mistaken.

'If you think I'm going to let you out of my sight for even a second,' he said, giving her a level look that was disturbingly knowing in an altogether different kind of way, 'you can think again.'

'That's a ridiculous overreaction.' Mia stepped past him, out into the cold, and shivered as the freezing air hit her cheeks. 'Anyone would think you don't trust me.'

'I don't. At least, not to put your feet up and rest.'

'Why not?'

'Because you're as ambitious, driven and dedicated as I am,' he said. 'In your situation, I might start wondering what the fuss had been about and be planning a quick trip to the office to make sure that everything was all right.'

Despite the cold, her entire body heated. The man was annoyingly perceptive. 'The idea never crossed my mind.'

'Didn't it?'

'I care as much as you obviously do about the health of this baby, Zander. I'm not going to do anything stupid.'

'I hope not,' he said, stamping his feet and blowing on his hands. 'Which is why you'll agree to move in with me.'

'That *would* be stupid.'

'Who will look after you if you go home alone?'

'I don't need looking after. I can rest on my own. I'll be fine.'

'I disagree.'

He took her elbow, as if he feared she might slip perhaps, but she wasn't geriatric and his touch did odd things to her equilibrium so she shook herself free. With a barely concealed huff of exasperation, Zander set off for the car and she followed, her breath condensing into little puffs of clouds as she trotted along beside him.

'What makes you think you would be the best person for the job anyway?' she said, nevertheless rather glad when he adjusted his long stride to match her shorter one. 'Do you have any caring experience?'

'None at all. But is there anyone else?'

No. But that was beside the point. 'Wouldn't you have work to do?'

'I will work from home,' he said, as if it were a fait accompli, which it most certainly was *not*. 'And when I cannot, I will delegate.'

'Would you be ready to curtail your social life too?'

'What makes you think it needs curtailing?'

'You've been out practically every night since we—' she broke off, flushing at the memory of exactly what they'd done together, then finished '—created this situation.'

'How do you know that?'

'I've seen the photos.'

The gleam that flashed in his eyes did all sorts of things it shouldn't to her insides. 'Have you been checking up on me?'

Maybe. Because frustratingly, despite removing him from her phone, despite *knowing* that what they'd had had been one night only, she hadn't been able to get him out of her head. She'd succumbed to temptation irritatingly quickly but googling his name and then being confronted with dozens of images of him at parties and dinners and events, invariably with a beautiful woman hanging off his arm, hadn't done her any favours so she'd forced herself to stop.

'Not at all,' she lied smoothly. 'The reports of your comings and goings are hard to avoid, that's all.'

'*I* manage to avoid them,' he observed dryly

as the car lit up like a Christmas tree at their approach.

'So much for me ruining you for anyone else,' she said, not that she'd ever believed she had because she wasn't a complete idiot. 'But I tell you what *would* ruin you. Or at least your reputation. A flatmate, pregnant with your baby.'

'Let me worry about that.'

Mia watched Zander stride around the car towards the passenger seat door, and thought, hah. As if. When had she ever let someone else worry about anything? For as long as she could remember the worry had been all hers. Her mother's rapidly deteriorating health. The threat of social services turning up and taking her away. Money, food, school. Her business, her future, her *life*. She couldn't imagine having nothing to worry about at all.

'How would you see it playing out?' she asked, not that she was particularly interested or anything.

'The baby is my responsibility,' he said, opening the door and standing to one side. 'I will do everything in my power to keep it safe. And therefore you too. I'll get the world's top obstetrician on speed dial. You'll be waited on hand and foot. You won't have to lift a finger. You can avail yourself of my library and my cinema. Your comfort will be my only concern. Anything you want, anything you need, tell me and I will arrange it. Your wish will be my command.'

He stopped and in the ensuing silence Mia thought with a sigh of longing that actually that did all sound really rather heavenly. When was the last time she'd been taken care of? She couldn't remember. The first signs of her mother's dementia had begun the summer after she'd turned eleven, even though they hadn't had a formal diagnosis until much later, and from that moment on, for the next five years, their roles had slowly reversed.

Mia was the one who'd kept everything together while her mother became increasingly incapable. She'd done the shopping, the cleaning, the washing and the cooking. She'd got rid of nosy neighbours and come up with endless plausible excuses for not being at school. She'd done whatever it had taken to keep up the pretence that everything was all right because she'd been terrified of having to confront the unknowns and uncertainties of reality. And as if that hadn't been enough, she'd done it all while struggling to work out what was happening to the mother she adored, who sometimes adored her back and sometimes didn't, who was sometimes lucid and sometimes wasn't, which had been bewildering and scary and heartbreaking.

So why was she resisting Zander's proposal when being cared for and not having to worry about a thing had once been the stuff of her dreams?

Because it was more of a command than a suggestion and she was used to being in control of her life? Because of the annoying way she still responded to him? Because after nearly two decades of fending for herself she suspected she might actually find the attention a bit stifling?

Well, she should probably get used to occasionally relinquishing control if they were going to parent together, and her reaction to him needn't be an issue. She'd spent the four months prior to his party ignoring it. She could do so for another couple of weeks. No doubt the searing attraction she still felt was down to rampaging hormones anyway, but all she had to do if it did become a problem was remind herself that he'd once blocked her phone, a sure sign if ever there was one that he was absolutely not interested in a repeat of the night they'd spent together.

They were going to be connected for years.

They needed to get to know each other, and wouldn't that be easier if they were in the same vicinity? Wouldn't a short period of cohabitation provide an excellent opportunity to discuss the future? He could hardly move in with her. She only had the one bedroom. If she did feel a bit smothered, she could find ways to sneak out, she was sure. Presumably he wouldn't be there *all* the time. And the library and cinema did sound intriguing.

'How many bedrooms do you have?' she asked because if she was going to do this it seemed prudent to check the sleeping arrangements.

'There are three guest suites, of which you can take your pick.'

Excellent. 'What's your kitchen like?'

'Pristine. Enormous. State-of-the-art and very well equipped.'

'May I use it?'

'It would be all yours.'

'All right, then,' she said, and got in the car.

CHAPTER SIX

HAVING INSTRUCTED HIS assistants to cancel his plans for the rest of the week, Zander moved Mia and her luggage into his central London penthouse apartment that evening. He wasn't taking any chances. In the six months since they'd met, he hadn't known her to sit still or stop moving once. He'd detected a certain shiftiness in her demeanour outside the clinic, which suggested that, left to her own devices, she might make unwise decisions. Besides, the sooner she was safely installed in one of his guest rooms, he'd figured, the sooner he could start changing her mind about marriage.

With hindsight, however, he should have given some thought to what happened beyond that short-term goal because now he'd got her here, for the first time since he could remember, he was at a loss as to how to proceed.

Generally, the women in his life fell into one

of three categories—family member, colleague or business acquaintance, object of his desire—and generally, he had no trouble adapting his behaviour to suit the occasion. When it came to his sisters, he rolled with the punches. At work, he treated everyone with equal decisiveness and respect. His seduction technique was second to none and he could operate the app that controlled the lights in this apartment, which had no fewer than nine settings that mostly ranged from low to off, with his eyes closed.

Mia, however, was in a category all of her own, for which there were no guidelines, and he had the suspicion that this experience was going to be like stumbling around uncharted territory in the dark with neither a compass nor a torch.

'Is there anything in particular you need?' he asked, setting down her one suitcase and her overnight bag just inside the guest room door.

'No, this looks amazingly comfortable,' she said as she swept her gaze around the space and then headed to one of the floor-to-ceiling triple-glazed windows. 'Very soothing, all these neutrals. Great views in the daylight, I imagine.'

The views were indeed excellent. This bedroom overlooked Hyde Park on one side and on another Green Park and beyond, all the way to the City. At a push, on a very clear day, you could even see the sixty-storey Stanhope Kallis tower in Canary Wharf, where she'd changed his life for ever.

However, Zander wasn't remotely interested in the views. Every drop of willpower he possessed was engaged in keeping his attention off the enormous bed that dominated the space and resisting the onslaught of the hot, vivid memories that brought to mind what had happened the last time he and Mia had been in such proximity to one.

Sex was *not* what this arrangement was about, he reminded himself sternly as he willed his pulse to slow and the fire scorching through him to ease. It was about keeping Mia and his baby safe and securing the future. A purely practical plan, the only kind he knew how to make, the kind he excelled at.

So he would not think about the electrifying heat of her mouth, the dazzling strength of her desire for him and the way he'd repeatedly lost his mind in her arms. He would not dwell on the irritating way the details kept haunting his dreams by night and derailing his thoughts by day, or the knee-buckling attraction that inconveniently still burned as brightly as it ever had.

Nor would he allow himself to revisit the

events of this afternoon and his utterly unfathomable response to her panicked phone call. What that suffocating pressure in his chest and the hollowing out of his stomach had been about he had no idea. He hadn't felt anything like it in decades. But it required no analysis. In the general scheme of things, it was unimportant.

What *was* important was coming up with another of those purely practical plans pretty damn quickly, because how was he going to get through the next two weeks if every time he looked at her he was struck by the overwhelming urge to flatten her against the nearest suitable surface and keep her there until his hunger was satisfied and she couldn't move? He'd go mad. It had to stop.

Thanks to his once-only rule, Mia could no longer be the object of his desire and she certainly wasn't a family member, so perhaps the way forward was to treat her like a business acquaintance.

Respect.

Casual interest.

Charm.

Could that be the right approach? Absolutely. Because there was no other. And who knew? She might even welcome it. She gave no indication that she was similarly tormented by an ongoing attraction, but if she was and her reluctance to move in had not been about a loss of independence at all, then proceeding in this way would be win-win.

There'd have to be conversation, of course. His apartment was large but ensuring her comfort and their baby's safety would naturally necessitate interaction and he liked silence as much as he liked being on his own, in other words, not at all. In the absence of company and activity, his thoughts tended to circle round his faults and his worth—or obvious lack thereof—and he preferred to dwell on neither. Small talk generally made him want to grind his teeth because it was such a waste of time, but here and now it might be exactly the thing.

'What would you like for supper?' he said, practically sagging with relief at having found a way to handle his unexpected and very disturbing house guest.

'I'll eat anything,' she said with a quick smile that for a second made him think of the bed before he told himself sternly, *Business acquaintance...business acquaintance*. 'Although all the good stuff like blue cheese and shellfish is off the menu for a while.'

He obliterated the impulse to take several

forward and took a decisive step back instead. 'Right. I'll leave you to settle in,' he said with a nod.

'Thank you.'

'Come down when you're ready.'

It took Mia more time to shower and change than it did to unpack. She hadn't brought much because she wouldn't be staying long. Once her clothes were stowed in the walk-in wardrobe and her toiletries lined up in the limestone-tiled shower room, she called Hattie for the fourth time since leaving the clinic for assurance that everything was on track for the party this evening, then ventured back down the wide floating staircase.

Unsurprisingly, the vast living space of Zander's penthouse apartment, which occupied the three top floors of London's most exclusive residential address, was very masculine—all moody colours, bold lines and a stark absence of daintiness, much like the man himself.

It was also, clearly, a party pad.

At one end of the room, above a granite fireplace that looked as if it was rarely used, hung the largest TV she'd ever seen. In front of the grate, three steel and leather sofas were arranged around a glass coffee table, together with a pair of armchairs that suggested style trumped comfort. In the middle of the space stood a full-size pool table, its petrol blue baize the only shot of colour in a palette of dark, sensuous neutrals, and at the other end was a bar area that stretched along the entire length of the wall, where dozens of bottles lined up on the softly lit shelves behind a counter large enough to accommodate half a dozen stools.

Arriving at the bottom of the stairs, Mia assessed the brown and gold colour scheme and the natural but hard surfaces, similar in style to upstairs, although way more intense, and decided that the décor wasn't to her taste at all. She preferred brighter colours and a wider variety of them. She liked a curtain and a cushion or two and favoured easy comfort over sophisticated style. The only softness to be found here was in the thick cream rugs that covered the dark wood floor. The pictures on the walls were large and abstract. The books on the coffee table were hardbacked showpieces. Even the lamps dotted around the room had a sculptural air about them.

And where were the photos, the evidence of the people in his life? Admittedly, she only had one—of her and her mother, taken at the Herschel Museum of Astronomy that they'd visited the summer before she'd become ill—but Zander had five siblings and a mother, a smattering of in-laws and a clutch of nieces and nephews. If she'd been lucky enough to have a family the size of his, her bookcases would be buckling beneath the number and weight of the frames.

However, what her host chose to surround himself with was none of her concern. *She* didn't have to live in this lavish yet strangely soulless apartment. She was just a temporary guest. And presumably not the first, although how many women he'd entertained here and in what way wasn't any of her business either. No. She couldn't care less about what he'd got up to in the days since their one-night stand. So what if he *had* slept with all the women he'd been pictured with? The future was what was important, not the past.

After a quick look in first the study—no photos in there either—and then the dining room that could seat twenty, Mia eventually found Zander in the kitchen where, beyond the mile-long island, he was transferring silver-cloche-covered dishes from a trolley onto a round marble table encircled by four brass-framed and black velvet-covered chairs.

'How are you feeling?' he said, glancing up with those darkly compelling eyes of his that never failed to make her tingle in places she shouldn't.

'Fine.'

'Any pain? Any twinges?'

'No.' At least, not of the kind he was referring to, thank goodness. Plenty of throbbing in other places though. He'd swapped his suit for faded jeans and a white shirt, which emphasised his Greek heritage, and looked even more gorgeous than he had in full billionaire businessman mode, striding around the hospital demanding answers.

'Let me know immediately if that changes.'

'I will.'

'Take a seat.'

Doing as he suggested at one of the laid places in order not to ogle him, Mia surveyed the space with a professional eye. Along one wall, a two-plate oven-microwave combination was built into a bank of sleek graphite units. To her right, a full height wine fridge held what had to amount to three dozen bottles. There was ample storage and on the stainless-steel island only a gleaming hob and a sparkling sink broke up the acres of worktop. As he'd assured her earlier, it was state-of-the-art and pristine, and clearly not a lot of cooking went on in here.

'Something smells amazing,' she said, her

mouth watering as he lifted off the cloches to reveal a platter of what looked like roast cod with sides of crisp French beans and buttery baby new potatoes.

'The restaurant downstairs is the best in the city,' he said, dispensing with the silverware and then languidly folding himself into the seat opposite her. 'Help yourself.'

Mia picked up a fish slice and transferred a portion of cod from the platter to her plate. 'Do you ever cook?'

'Coffee and toast and that's about it,' he said, sitting back and watching her lazily. 'I'm out a lot of the time. When I'm here I order in.'

'How are you not the size of a house?'

'There's a gym and a pool in the basement.'

'You must be incredibly disciplined.'

'I am.'

And hadn't she reaped the benefit of it, she reflected as she added some beans and potatoes to the fish. From what she could recall of the night they'd spent together—and she could recall every single minute as if it were yesterday—his muscles really were something else: hard and defined, as if he'd been sculpted from warm marble.

And his strength, his power... That first time, in the nightclub cloakroom, he'd picked her up as if she'd weighed nothing and then held her against the wall with only his hands and the thrust of his hips. Once at her flat, there'd been sweat and breathlessness aplenty, but not from the effort of moving her into and keeping her in the positions they'd achieved.

His stamina had been impressive. His mouth a deliciously wicked thing that had instantly turned her into a puddle of need every time he put it on her. And she just had to *look* at his hands to remember them slowly and sensuously sliding over her skin.

The faultlessness of her memory was why she'd babbled on about the views from her room earlier, which she couldn't even see because it was dark. All she'd been able to think about was the enormous bed and the magical things he'd once done to her in hers. She'd had to move to the window before she'd forgotten she was only here because of the scare they'd had this afternoon, lost control and given in to the tidal wave of need that had rushed through her.

Even now, with him leaning forward to help himself, which sent a wave of his scent in her direction, it was a struggle to focus. In her mind's eye, she could see him pushing aside the crockery. Slowly getting to his feet and drawing her up and onto the table, where he'd gently push her back and feast on her until she was trembling all over and crying out and—

'What would you like to drink?'

His question shattered the silence like a shot and she jumped. She went hot. Her gaze flew up and collided with his, but his expression gave no indication that he knew what she'd been thinking, which was a relief because if he did she'd be mortified.

'Some sparkling water would be great,' she said, thinking that the next couple of weeks were going to be a lot tougher than she'd imagined if she couldn't get a handle on her response to him.

Zander got up and headed to the fridge. Mia flapped out her napkin to cool herself down, then laid it across her lap and took the opportunity to remind herself that the only context in which she should be thinking of her host was as the father of her child.

When he returned to the table, she took a much-needed sip of water and turned her attention to the food. The beautifully cooked cod flaked beneath the barest pressure of her knife. The beans were as bright green as they had been on the vine. Someone downstairs definitely knew what they were doing.

'What do you think of the food?' he asked,

and as the heat whipping around inside her dissipated Mia sent up a little prayer of thanks to the god of conversation.

'Delicious,' she said, using her fork to prod a potato that was neither too soft nor too hard but just perfect. 'The combination of chicory and seaweed with the cod is an interesting one. I might see if I can add something similar to the menus I offer. I'm always looking for new dishes.'

'You're exceptionally good at what you do.'

A ripple of pride shimmered through her. 'Thank you.'

'How did you get into it?'

'I left school at sixteen and went to catering college,' she said, figuring there was no time like the present for getting to know one another and they had to talk about *something*. 'I was there for two years and then took up an apprenticeship as a *chef de partie*. Six years ago, with eight years' training and experience under my belt, I set up my own business, which has gone from strength to strength ever since.'

He arched one dark eyebrow. 'That simple?'

If only. 'It's been anything but simple,' she said wryly. 'It's taken a lot of blood, sweat and tears to get where I am. It can be a brutal industry. The hours are horrendous and some of the chefs I worked for wouldn't last five minutes in an office. But I started cooking properly at the age of twelve and it's all I've wanted to do ever since.'

'Twelve is young.'

'My mother fell ill,' she said. 'She ended up needing a lot of care and because it was always just the two of us, it all fell on me. Cooking was my happy place when I didn't know what was going on but was terrified nonetheless.'

Zander twirled the stem of his wine glass between his fingers, the picture of casual interest. 'What happened?'

Abandoning her plate for a moment, Mia braced herself since it was still so difficult to talk about. 'The first sign that something was wrong was when she sent me into school on a Saturday, convinced it was a Friday,' she said with a sigh. 'Soon after that, her memory started failing and she couldn't find the words she wanted. She lost her job and once nearly set fire to the kitchen. I took over the cooking after that. I took over everything so that social services wouldn't find out about the situation and take me into care.'

'That must have been tough.'

'It was. Massively. Every day was a worry. I missed so much school. Money was impossibly tight. But the worst of it was seeing the mother I adored, who'd always fought my corner, disappear. We were so intense. It was always us against the world. And then it wasn't. As time went on, more often than not it became her against me and that was so devastating. Her mood swings were unpredictable and merciless. Some of the things she said cut through me like a knife and I was too young to fully understand what was going on.'

'Didn't anybody else?'

She shook her head. 'I got very good at lying and hiding to keep us together. I didn't want to be taken into care. Anyway. She was eventually diagnosed with rapid onset dementia. Whether the progression of the disease could have been slowed if she had had help is something I'll never know. I've learned to live with the guilt of that, but it was hard for a while.'

'You talk about her in the past.'

Mia swallowed hard. 'She went into hospital after falling and breaking her arm and caught a superbug which turned into sepsis. She never came home. I was sixteen when she died.'

'I'm so sorry.'

'So am I,' she said, her heart aching at the loss, even now after fourteen years. 'But I'd grieved for her long before that.'

'I can see why financial security would be so important to you.'

'Security in general is important to me.'

'Marry me and you'll have it,' he said, his dark, mesmerising gaze intent on hers but his expression otherwise blank. 'Marry me, Mia, and you'll never have to worry about anything ever again.'

CHAPTER SEVEN

THAT ZANDER HAD chosen that particular moment to push his agenda should not have stung quite as much as it did, Mia thought, stamping out the strange sense of hurt and disappointment and determinedly pulling herself together.

She should have known he wouldn't let the subject of marriage lie. Hadn't she already seen how tenacious and unyielding he could be when he wanted something? Didn't he have a reputation for ruthlessness? Why wouldn't he take advantage of her rare moment of vulnerability? It was probably her fault in the first place, for carelessly revealing such personal details and furnishing him with ammunition that he hadn't hesitated to use.

'We've already discussed this,' she said coolly, reminding herself to keep her wits about her before she was lulled into another false sense of security and quite possibly found herself at the altar.

'Not to my satisfaction.'

'My position on the subject remains unchanged.'

'So does mine.'

'Yes, I got that from the demand for my birth certificate.'

'Which you still haven't provided.'

Appetite gone, Mia pushed her plate to one side. 'You really do have a problem with trust, don't you?' she said, deciding that it was now his turn to talk. He might even reveal a vulnerability of his own that she could exploit. 'Is that why you're still single?'

Zander half got up, leaned over and reached for her plate. 'What makes you think that?'

'You're handsome, successful and rich, and you're thirty-five,' she replied, steeling herself against the temptation to close her eyes and breathe him in. 'Evolutionarily, you should have been snapped up years ago. There has to be some reason you aren't.'

'Perhaps I simply haven't wanted to be snapped up.'

'Ah, yes,' she said dryly. 'Too many women, too little time, I seem to recall.'

He gave a shrug and flashed her a smile

filled with self-deprecation that she didn't believe for a moment. 'Your words, not mine.'

'Yet you're willing to be hitched to me.'

'That's different,' he said, removing their plates to the trolley and returning with a beautiful blueberry tart. 'Our marriage will be purely one of convenience. A legality. Nothing more.'

'How romantic.'

'I'm not interested in romance.'

'What about love?'

He sat back down, frowning in obvious confusion, as if she were speaking Swahili. 'Love?'

'You know. The heart-thumping, giddy feeling that's generally considered to be the basis of a long-term union.'

'I can't think of anything worse,' he said with a tiny yet visible shudder as he picked up a cake slice.

'Why not?'

'What is there to admire about vulnerability and exposure and losing control?'

Mia didn't know quite how to respond to that. She'd never thought of it in those terms. Who would?

'That's quite an indictment,' she said after a moment, as taken aback by his cynical view on the subject as she was intrigued. 'Are you speaking from experience?'

'It's merely an observation,' he said, interestingly avoiding the question as he deftly cut the tart into eighths.

'In that case, love could just as easily be joy and contentment and finding strength and support in sharing the highs as well as the lows.'

'Only if you believe in fairy tales.'

'I do.'

'Why?'

'Because my mother's illness made life really hard and love got lost amongst all the fear and resentment and worry and confusion,' she said, deciding to pause her embargo on the disclosure of personal information in order to get her point across once and for all. 'At times, her cruelty and her dependency made me hate her, which I still feel sickeningly guilty about even though I know that none of what happened was anyone's fault. But the trauma of those five years means that now I crave love. I want to find my soulmate, someone to share my life with, to not feel lonely any more. Even more than I want success and financial security, in fact. And that's why I won't marry you simply for the sake of our child.'

'You're putting your needs first.'

She nodded. 'I am.' And there was nothing wrong with that.

'Finding your soulmate will be hard once the baby comes along and you're parenting with me,' he observed. 'We're going to be in each other's lives for years.'

'I know,' she agreed with a flurry of emotion that seemed to be an odd concoction of excitement, panic, exhilaration and terror. 'I realise that the obstacles littering my path to a happy ending are significant. But other people manage it and I refuse to give up hope.'

'You'll eventually come round to my way of thinking.'

'I won't.'

Zander waved aside Mia's offer of help with the clearing up and merely nodded when she coolly thanked him for supper, claimed exhaustion and bade him goodnight.

Having sent the dishes back downstairs, he poured himself a drink and took it into his study with the intention of catching up on work. After half an hour, however, he had to admit defeat because all he could think about was the meal they'd just shared and the complete and utter failure of his plan to consider her nothing more than a business acquaintance.

Firstly, he couldn't fathom ever understanding anyone who had such a delusional attitude to romantic relationships. He got why Mia might think she wanted one after the childhood experiences she'd had, and it was clear she found his opinion on the subject incomprehensible, but couldn't she see how risky it was to indulge emotion and potentially wind up exposed to immense torment and pain? How could she be so naïve? So trusting in something so fickle? It was a mystery, and she was a fool.

Secondly, it had become apparent as soon as they'd started talking that his interest in her was anything but casual. In response to the revelations about her upbringing he'd been gripped with the desire to know more. Shockingly, he'd felt a certain kinship with her on account of sharing the experience of having parents who were—or had been—physically or emotionally absent and feeling bewilderingly isolated despite existing in the company of others.

His curiosity did not need indulging, he'd had to remind himself sternly when it had been on the tip of his tongue to point the similarities out. There was no need whatsoever to compare and contrast the ways in which they'd grown up or to wish things could have been easier for her. Neither how she still felt about it nor her loneliness was any of his concern.

Developing that sort of a connection was not

what was required here, which was a relief because his experience with Valentina had proved that, for some reason he'd never been able to work out, he had zero ability to maintain such a thing anyway.

All that *was* required was a practical relationship based on the needs of their child, as he'd mentioned once he'd finally got a grip on the appalling, petrifying urge to share with her some stories of his own.

There was no earthly reason to confess that the reason he was so disciplined about food and exercise was because as a kid he'd eaten anything he could lay his hands on, which had had an inevitable effect, until he'd figured that a better, healthier way of dealing with his parents' lack of interest in him was to simply shut himself off from anything that hurt so nothing could ever bother him again.

Mia did not need to know that when *he* was twelve he'd spent most of his time trying to find out where his mother was, failing to comprehend why his father preferred to spend more time with his older brother than him and attempting to understand his siblings.

Perhaps it had been callous of him to bring marriage up so soon after she'd revealed so much that was so personal. Judging by the way she'd cooled in response, she'd certainly thought so. But the alternative—caving in to temptation and allowing her a glimpse into the emptiness of his soul—was infinitely worse.

Finally, and most worryingly, it had become increasingly obvious over the past couple of hours that although Mia could not be the object of his desire, given that he'd already slept with her, she still was.

Sitting across the table from her had been torture. Keeping his mind out of the gutter and his hands to himself had proved far harder than he'd envisaged. His attention had been repeatedly drawn to her mouth, which had conjured up uncomfortable memories of other things she could do with it. If he hadn't suddenly recalled his plan to engage in small talk and asked her if she wanted a drink, he might well have acted on the insistent desire drumming through him and carted her off to bed.

None of these discoveries were good, he thought darkly as he poured himself another generous measure of Metaxa. His rampant curiosity about her, the unexpected fragility of his guard, even his bizarre enjoyment of her defiance, were concerning. His one-night-only rule felt unacceptably under threat. The usual louche detachment with which he liked to approach life was deserting him.

So what was he going to do about it?

Despite his original intention to keep a very close eye on her, it seemed wise to temporarily put some distance between them until he'd got used to the situation and had his continuing desire for her under control.

But how was he to achieve that?

Simply holing up in his study here wouldn't work. She'd still be in the vicinity, moving around in his space, filling the air with her scent and tempting him to throw caution to the wind. How long would he last before the defences that had served him so well over the years crumbled beneath the weight of his need for her?

He'd have to go into the office instead. There he'd get the breathing space he needed. Workwise, that would be the right move too. Despite his assurances earlier that he could work from home and delegate if necessary, the thought of spending too long away from his desk made him jumpy. The shipping side of the company was launching a new cruise line and the plans were at a crucial stage. Decisions would be made far more efficiently if he were there.

He could still ensure Mia's comfort and mon-

itor her well-being, of course. She would still
be fed and watered and want for nothing. He'd
simply outsource her care instead of seeing to
it himself. It mattered not one jot who kept an
eye on her as long as she was safe, and he'd put
every resource he had—with the exception of
himself—at her disposal.

He wouldn't be gone for long. He'd soon get
everything under control and be back on track.
In fact, if she *was* suffering from the attraction
in the way he was, she might even welcome his
absence and some breathing space of her own.

It was another excellent plan, he thought with
satisfaction as he stared out at the twinkling
Christmas lights of Knightsbridge and drained
his glass. And this time it would work.

Contrary to his assumption, Mia did not welcome Zander's absence.

Once again, she'd gone to sleep in his vicinity and woken up late to an empty apartment
but, unlike before, he'd left a note.

She discovered it on the island in the kitchen,
into which she'd ventured after recovering from
the lingering nausea, showering and dressing.
Apparently, an urgent meeting had called him
into the office, but the concierge would help
with anything she needed, the restaurant down-

stairs would send lunch up at one and his driver would take her wherever she wanted to go. Zander would be in touch later, but in the meantime she was to put her feet up and relax.

Mia frowned down at the note, not a little put out. Last night as she'd been getting ready for bed, not only had she vowed to ignore the clearly one-sided attraction but also she'd decided to be less sensitive and more pragmatic about the situation. To adopt *his* approach, in fact. To that end, she'd been looking forward to quizzing him about himself over breakfast. She wanted to know more about his family, his work, and explore his fascinating opinions about love.

That, now, would not be happening. However, she was not going to let it overly bother her. Presumably, being CEO of a giant global company meant that delegating took time and she imagined that not all meetings could be done virtually. No doubt he'd had to leave early and hadn't wanted to wake her. At some point today he'd be back, surely, and as it was less than twenty-four hours since the scare that had landed her here, she probably ought to take this opportunity to consider their baby and do as he suggested.

So, after a cup of green tea and some crackers, magicked up by Tony, the obliging concierge at the front desk, Mia spent an hour analysing her spreadsheets. She then called Hattie to check that everything was on track for the dinner party this evening and answered some emails.

At eleven, she wrapped up warm and took a walk. At one, she had lunch—a melt-in-the-mouth quiche followed by a creamy lemon mousse that exploded her taste buds and had her taking notes. Following a brief nap, she headed downstairs to check out the well-stocked library and fourteen-seat cinema, then googled how to play pool and put what she'd learned into practice.

By six in the evening, however, having run out of things to do and heard not a word from Zander, despite the declaration that he'd be in touch, Mia frowned into the empty fridge as she contemplated dinner, and wondered if she should message him.

Would an enquiry into his plans come across as needy? A bit on the clingy side? She'd faced that accusation a number of times before and had pledged to be more circumspect when it came to relationships, but no, this was an entirely different situation. They were equals and she had every right to want to know what the father of her child was up to, especially when she was here at his insistence. Besides, communication was going to be key in the future and she might as well start now, so she closed the fridge door and fished out her phone to text him.

Hope all's going well. Will you be back in time for supper? I could cook.

His reply came a few minutes later.

Back late. Don't wait up.

At the bald words—and the message they conveyed—Mia's eyebrows shot up. Well. That was an unexpected development. Hadn't he made a very firm point about not trusting her to rest and therefore needing to keep watch over her at all times?

But perhaps something unavoidable had come up, something that trumped his lack of trust, like the sinking of a ship or a scandal at the bank. Or maybe delegating and arranging to work from home was proving easier said than done. Whatever it was, she wasn't going to stress about it. She could ask him in the morning, along with all the other questions she had piling up.

In the meantime, she thought as she exited the kitchen and headed for the stairs, since she was exhausted, despite having achieved very little and not at all hungry after lunch, she was going to take his advice and get an early night.

Unfortunately for Mia's plans to find out what lay behind Zander's absence that day and get to know him better over breakfast, the next forty-eight hours followed a similar pattern to the first twenty-four.

During that time, she saw neither hide nor hair of him. Did he even return to the apartment at night? There was no evidence to suggest he did. They communicated entirely by text, she with increasing irritation and confusion, he with a frustrating lack of urgency and brevity. How long did it take to sort out working from home? she wondered with growing resentment as she tried to keep herself occupied without losing her mind. What was keeping him so busy? Was it *just* work, as he claimed?

She took endless walks. She made the mistake of visiting the department store down the road, which, two weeks before Christmas, had been a bunfight. She read two books and watched five films. By the afternoon of day three, however, having organised into alphabetical order the bottles on the shelves behind the bar—a new low—she'd had enough.

The situation had become wholly unacceptable, she thought, tight-jawed, as she read yet another obfuscating message and her patience, stretched to its absolute limit, finally snapped.

What on earth was going on?

She frequently didn't hear from him for hours. She hadn't seen him in days. What had happened to his alleged concern for the welfare of her and their baby? That had been the whole point of moving her in, and he'd been so resolute, yet almost immediately it seemed to have fallen off his radar. Had she been wrong about his paternal instincts? Mistaken about his ability to step up should something happen to her? And what about seeing to her every need?

How were they supposed to get to know each other and discuss the future if he wasn't around? What the hell had been the point of installing her here in the first place if he'd been intending to abandon her all along? What was he *thinking*?

None of these questions she could answer—and she point blank refused to entertain thoughts about where he was at night, what he got up to and who he did it with because that only tied her in ridiculously jealous knots—but as her frustration and resentment mounted, of one thing she was certain: she was done with sitting here twiddling her thumbs until he finally deigned to grace her with his presence. She was climbing the walls. She couldn't stand being so unproductive. She needed to keep busy, to constantly move forward, not stagnate like this, passive and idle.

Why were the sacrifices all hers? Why should he get to work and she not? At this very minute Hattie and the team were arranging canapés on trays in readiness for a private view at a cutting-edge art gallery. The client was new and influential. Her reputation was on the line, and she'd been twitching all day about not being there in person.

These past few days, she'd managed to control her anxiety about staying away from her business in order to play her part in their arrangement but now she was thinking—if Zander was going to renege on his side of the deal, then why on earth should she continue to bother with hers? She felt absolutely fine. She'd experienced no more pain, no more spotting. The gallery was only a ten-minute walk from here and when they'd swung by her flat to pick up a bag the afternoon she'd moved in, she'd packed her black dress, just in case. There was nothing stopping her from dropping in to make sure things were going smoothly. She could be there and back in a couple of hours. And not that it mattered in the slightest, but Zander would never even know.

CHAPTER EIGHT

'SHE'S DOING *WHAT*?'

In response to Tony the concierge's bomb-shell, Zander nearly dropped his phone.

'Miss Halliday just left,' Tony repeated slowly and loudly, as if Zander's hearing was somehow impaired rather than merely succumbing to outrage and shock. 'And when I asked her where she was going, as per your instructions, she mentioned popping to a gallery around the corner. I understand that her company is catering an event there. A private viewing, she said. We had a very interesting conversation about modern art and the food she designed to accompany it.'

Zander didn't give a toss about modern art. Or designer food. He did, however, object greatly to Mia taking advantage of his absence to do what they'd agreed she wouldn't.

'Many thanks for the update, Tony,' he muttered, then hung up and leapt to his feet.

What the hell was she playing at? he wondered as he grabbed his coat and strode to the lift. Did she have no concern at all for the safety of the child she was carrying? Short walks and a brief trip to the shops were one thing. Defying his orders to go to work and most likely overdoing it—because why wouldn't she give an event she'd planned anything less than one hundred percent?—was quite another. How could she be so selfish?

With every step he took his anger climbed, but it wasn't solely directed at her. Much as he'd like not to, he had to accept part of the blame for what had happened, which only added fuel to the fire.

He shouldn't have stayed away so long. He hadn't planned to. He'd assumed a day would be more than enough to get a grip on his unruly reaction to her, but then she'd texted him, offering to cook, and with the previous meal's struggles fresh in his mind, he'd thought it wise to maintain his distance a little while longer. A little while stretched into a longer while, with regular updates from Tony assuring him she was fine, but once again the plan that had seemed such a solid one at the time had *not* worked out as he'd hoped.

So much for out of sight, out of mind, he thought darkly as he stalked to his car. Despite his hopes to the contrary, Mia occupied his thoughts all the damn time. At night, while he tossed and turned in the bedroom suite that connected to his office, she invaded his dreams and destroyed his peace. By day, thoughts of what she was doing and how she was derailed his focus so severely it was a miracle he hadn't seriously screwed up.

As he fired up the powerful engine and steered the low-slung convertible out of the car park, he tried, and failed, to work out what it was about her that was so all-consuming, so distracting. Yes, she was beautiful and sexy, but so were many women and he'd met a lot of them. Could it be the fact that she was carrying his baby, which was sparking in him some primitive instinct to defend and protect, even though he wasn't doing a very good job of it at the moment? Or was it simply down to the unsettling novelty of never having had a guest who'd stayed longer than one night?

Whatever it was, spending the last three days at his desk and away from her had not suppressed anything. He had not got his desire

for her under control at all. His defences felt as
rocky as ever and he was more on edge than he
could remember.

The tiny voice in his head, the one which a
moment ago had prompted a rare reflection on
his role in this debacle, was now urging him to
exercise extreme caution. He was in a febrile
state. He wasn't thinking clearly. But it was far
too late for that. The decision to go home and
confront her had been sealed the minute he'd
heard what she was up to. Wild horses wouldn't
drag him from it now, because Mia had some
serious explaining to do.

Two hours after she'd left, Mia let herself back
into the apartment. She toed off her shoes with
a sigh of relief and headed for the stairs, adrenalin still whooshing around her system like
wildfire.

What a night.

What an event.

Celebrities had abounded. Champagne had
flowed and canapés had been devoured. Within
half an hour every piece that hung on the walls
had had a little red dot on its label.

Quite frankly, she hadn't understood the art
at all and had liked it even less, but if someone wanted to spend a cool two million on a

blue circle with a red line through it, that was up to them. She was hardly going to complain. The enormous amounts of money that moved around this city financed the catering and gave her a job she loved.

She didn't regret dropping in for a moment. Hattie had been faintly put out to see her, true, and she was tired and her feet hurt, but she'd felt so *alive*, so full of purpose. The event had been a resounding success. The effusive gallery owner had said she'd be recommending Halliday Catering to everyone she knew. Tomorrow, there was a lunch in the Docklands for which her company was supplying the food and she'd be going to that too.

'Good evening.'

At the low rumbling voice that came from the depths of the living space, Mia froze for a second then spun round to see Zander behind the bar, in the shadows, fixing himself a drink.

Her head emptied. Her heart lurched and then began to pound. Heat poured through her and her cheeks flamed, as if she'd been caught in the act. But she had nothing whatsoever to feel guilty about. If anyone did, it was him for having got her here under false pretences and then abandoning her. So she took a deep breath and willed herself to calm down.

'Goodness, you gave me a fright,' she said, nevertheless needing a moment to gather her wits and stamp out the inconvenient surge of desire that the sight of him always provoked, even now when she was so annoyed with him.

'My apologies.'

'What are you doing here?' How ironic that he should show up the very evening she'd gone out.

He pulled off the top of a bottle that contained an amber liquid, a shot of which he poured into a tumbler. 'I live here, if I remember correctly.'

'You could have fooled me.'

The only indication that her jibe had hit its mark was a minute clenching of his jaw. He slowly and pointedly ran his dark gaze over her, taking in the dress she wore and the file she carried, obviously putting two and two together, and she flushed—ridiculously—all over again.

'You've been to work.'

In response to his accusation, she bristled and lifted her chin. 'And?'

'You said you'd stay away from your business.'

That was rich, coming from him. 'Yes, well, *you* said you'd work from home,' she countered, padding to the bar because, for her at least, this conversation had been brewing for days and she wanted to be able to see every single reaction.

'Is that what this was, then? A tit-for-tat?'

'Of course not. I'm not that petty. This was me having had enough of being treated so shabbily, of being the only one around here making any sacrifices at all and doing something to stop myself going completely out of my mind with boredom.'

A flicker of what she hoped was guilt flared in the dark depths of his eyes, but all too soon his expression reverted to uncompromising.

'Was it worth taking a risk on the safety of our baby?'

What? That was a bit much. 'I wasn't risking anything.'

'Only a few days ago you thought you were miscarrying,' he said, the simmering anger she could now feel emanating from him tightening his voice. 'On the advice of the doctor, you are supposed to be resting.'

'And I have been resting,' she said, her own temper stirring in response to his wholly outrageous ire. 'For *days*. But I'm not used to lounging around and doing nothing. I'm not an invalid. I feel absolutely fine. And I'm not going to sit here gathering dust while you waltz off to do whatever it is you've been doing. I have no clue why you'd vanish at the first available opportunity when you were so adamant about not letting me out of your sight, and you can work from dawn until dusk and then party the night away with whoever you like, for all I care. What I will say, however, is that your recent behaviour certainly won't make me more amenable to marriage. And if this is the way things are going to be from now on, then what's the point of me being here at all?'

A tiny muscle twitched in his cheek. 'The point,' he said stonily, 'is that with you here at least *someone* will be looking out for your welfare and that of our child.'

'Who?' she challenged. 'Because it obviously won't be you.'

'I've had someone keeping an eye on you.'

At that Mia reeled. What? The only person she'd interacted with at all had been the concierge.

'Tony?' she said, thinking of the many conversations they'd had and feeling absurdly betrayed. 'He's your informant?'

Zander, whose presence here this evening, she now realised, was clearly no coincidence, didn't like the implication that he'd been spying on her. She could tell by the way his jaw set and his eyes narrowed, but she didn't much like his underhand tactics so that was just too bad.

'It was important to me to know that you and the baby were all right,' he said tightly.

'But not important enough to take care of it yourself.'

'My absence was unavoidable.'

'For *three days*?'

'Why? Did you miss me?'

Yes. Bizarrely, she *had* missed him. She *hated* the thought of him partying the night away with who knew who. The days—and the nights—had been so long, so frustrating. But that wasn't the point.

'Your implication that I'm irresponsible is disgraceful,' she said hotly. 'The best person to decide how I am is me. It's certainly not you, either in person or by proxy. And know this, Zander Stanhope. I'm not going to languish in this bachelor pad of yours just because you demand it. And how would you keep me here anyway? By handcuffing me to the bed?'

His eyes glinted. A flash of colour flared across his cheekbones. 'It's an idea.'

Time seemed to slam to a halt. The image that flew into her head dried her mouth and sent shivers racing up and down her spine. Her temperature rocketed and her lungs collapsed and the fiery antagonism that was swirling between them morphed into something more sensuous, something darker, something entirely more thrilling.

'And what would you do with me then?' she asked, heart pounding, chin up, shoulders back, a lot more breathless than she'd have wished.

'What would you want me to do with you?' he said, his voice appearing to have dropped an octave.

'I'd want you to hand me the key so I could unlock myself and then get out of the room.'

'Would you?'

No. She'd want him to spread her out and have his wicked way with her until she was boneless and trembling. She'd want him to do to her everything she dreamed of at night, despite his recent shoddy behaviour. But she would not succumb. Seduction came as naturally to him as breathing, and she'd already fallen for it once. Besides, she was still furious with him. 'Absolutely.'

'So why do I get the feeling you're lying?'

'I have no idea,' she shot back. 'But I can assure you I'm not.'

Without warning, he banged his glass down with enough force to make her jump and planted his hands wide apart on the bar. 'Do you want to know why I've really stayed away from you for so long?' he practically growled, his eyes locking with hers, the intensity of their connection pinning her to the stool.

'You said it was work,' she managed, her entire body on fire in response to both his intoxicating proximity and the unexpected passion of his outburst.

'It wasn't work.'

'No?'

'It was because I can't get you out of my head.'

At his gritted confession, she stared at him for one frozen moment, her eyes wide, her mouth forming a little O of shock. 'What?'

'You've been in there since the moment we met,' he said, eyes blazing. 'I assumed taking you to bed would cure me of my fixation. That normally scratches the itch. But not in your case. You refuse to leave. Every time I look at you, I'm gripped with the urge to pull you into my arms and kiss you senseless. Every time I think of you, I develop an erection that *hurts*. The last three days—which, for your information, I have spent either at my desk or in the bedroom suite attached to my office and *not* partying—have been torture. Even now, when I'm furious with you, all I can think about is stripping that dress off you and doing to you what I did the last time I saw you wearing it.'

He stopped. Mia closed her mouth and released a breath before her lungs exploded.

'You want me?' she said, struggling to process the realisation that the attraction was not just on her side.

'I have never not wanted you,' he grated. 'You're driving me to distraction. Right now, I'm so hard it's possible I may suffer a permanent injury.'

'That's quite a line.'

'I very much wish it was.'

His obvious frustration implied that this wasn't a casual attempt to seduce. He wanted her against his will. Which was fascinating, but something to be analysed later because if he wanted her as much as she wanted him, stayed away because he didn't trust *himself* instead of not trusting *her*, then that changed everything.

'Yes, well, I can empathise,' she replied dazedly, her head spinning as she raked her gaze over the navy suit that emphasised his broad shoulders and lean physique and the white shirt open at the neck, which contrasted devastatingly with his olive skin and dark hair and eyes. 'I feel the same way about you. I can't forget the night we spent together either and, believe me, I've tried. At dinner the other evening I kept imagining you sweeping everything off the table and devouring me instead. Even though you left me here to moulder and I've been so annoyed and frustrated with you, I haven't been able to stop thinking about you. The nights are the worst.'

'It's unacceptable,' he said, a muscle clenching in his cheek.

'It's certainly uncomfortable,' she agreed, the desire pummelling through her robbing her of every thought except one. 'But there is an alternative solution to fleeing to the office and hiding out there whenever it gets too much to bear.'

'And what is that?'

'We could just have sex again.'

Complete silence followed that. For a moment or two Zander simply stared at her as if she'd sprouted horns. Then his brows snapped together and he gave his head a shake, clearly unable to believe what he was hearing. 'Are you mad?'

'I'm heading that way, hence the suggestion.'

'It's ridiculous.'

Quite possibly. Their situation was complicated enough as it was. However, it had become apparent that things couldn't go on as they were. Neither of them would survive.

The tension had to be defused somehow. And what was his problem? Wasn't he all about no-strings-attached sex? If anyone was to have had an issue with it, it should have been her. But she didn't. She was all for some unencumbered action. Anything to release the pressure she'd been feeling for days. She'd handled one night with him with equanimity. Why not two?

'I disagree,' she said, refusing to be intimidated by his incredulous intransigence. 'Unless we do something about this wild attraction, it's always going to be between us. It's going to make life even more difficult than it already is. It's only been three days and look at us. I'm not sure distance will provide much in the way of relief. We can't avoid each other for ever. In my opinion, it needs addressing, and sooner rather than later.'

'No,' he countered, jaw set in rebuttal, his dark eyes unusually stormy.

'Why not?'

'I won't allow it.'

'Because?'

'I have a once-only rule.'

Her eyebrows shot up. 'A what?'

'I only sleep with a woman once.'

'Seriously?'

'I don't want a relationship.'

He'd told her that before and she hadn't questioned it at the time, but now she was temporarily lost for words.

'Are you saying that you're so irresistible that two nights or more with you and a woman might get the wrong idea?' she asked, taken aback by the sheer arrogance of that because, though he'd demonstrated instances of that particular character trait before, this took it to a whole new level.

'I prefer not to put it to the test.'

'Since when?'

'Long enough to know it's a policy that serves me well.'

'What are you afraid of?'

'Nothing.'

Rubbish. He appeared to be afraid of clingy women at the very least, and she knew all about those because she, with her previous tendency to start picking out curtains a mere week into a relationship, used to be one of them. But while that definitely merited further investigation, now was not the time. Now was the time to get him to see things her way and satisfy the longing that throbbed inside her.

'Our situation is unique,' she said, holding his gaze, leaning a little into his space. 'I'm not one of your casual hook-ups. At least, not any longer. So the usual rules don't apply. I certainly wouldn't read anything into another night of sex with you. I'm not going to get the wrong idea. It would be a physical release, nothing more, and one which you obviously need as much as I do.'

'It's too dangerous.'

'Not from a medical point of view. The doctor said it would be fine.' She tilted her head and regarded him thoughtfully. 'Or is it me that's dangerous?'

'Don't be absurd,' he said through gritted teeth, looking as if he was resisting the urge to reach for her.

'I'm not the one being absurd,' she said in exasperation, disappointed, thwarted, but knowing that there was a fine line between persuading him to see sense and harassment. 'But OK. Stick your head in the sand if you want. I'm going up to bed. You know where to find me when you realise I'm right.'

Fists clenched, muscles so tight he feared they might snap, Zander watched Mia saunter off to the stairs, her shoes dangling from her fingers and her hips swinging in pure temptation, and thought that she was wrong. Dead wrong. The chemistry that burned between them would fizzle out. It had to. Even if he didn't have the rule by which he'd lived almost his entire adult life, sleeping with her again was a terrible idea. She might not read anything into it, but what if he did?

If he was being brutally honest with himself—a rare event, he'd be the first to admit—she'd never been a casual hook-up. That had certainly been the intention when he'd initially decided to hire her catering services, but it had swiftly turned into something different. Why else would he have pursued her when it had become apparent that the odds of success were zero?

It hadn't just been a reluctance to fail. Over the months, he'd come to admire her brain, her ambition and her drive to succeed as much as he was dazzled by her looks. The snippets of information about her that he hadn't sought but had acquired nonetheless—favourite colour yellow, go to comfort food spaghetti carbonara—had piqued his interest before he'd belatedly reminded himself that his interest had no business being piqued.

He was less enamoured with her levels of perceptiveness, however. Especially now, with the way that the question *But could she be right?* was pushing out everything else from his head. He didn't want to contemplate the implications of that. The notion that his reluctance to act on his desire for her could drive them apart and ruin his plans to bind her and their child to him permanently tightened his chest like a vice. Where would such an outcome leave him? Wandering alone through the wasteland that was the moral high ground, that was where, most probably.

He didn't appreciate the niggling suspicion that he hadn't really thought she'd put their baby in danger this evening but had subconsciously been waiting for an excuse to return to her. He didn't like the fact that he wanted her so much he hadn't been able to stop himself confessing it when he should have been remonstrating with her regardless.

But apparently she wanted him equally fiercely and, quite frankly, he didn't know how much more he could take. Why was he putting himself through the wringer like this? It was true that he never went back, but this was different. *She* was different.

So what on earth was he doing? It wasn't as if he was going to fall under her spell. He was far too disciplined for that. But his strategy for dealing with his desire for her clearly wasn't working, so what did he have to lose from testing hers? His life was hardly going to implode if he surrendered to one more night. Unless he completely lost his mind, which he wouldn't, it would still be just sex.

Ignoring his conscience, which was commanding him to stop the insanity *this instant*, to stick to the plan that had served him so well for nearly two decades because it suspected she could turn out to be very dangerous indeed, every cell of his body now taut with purpose and anticipation, Zander pushed himself off the counter, stalked round the bar and barked, 'Wait.'

CHAPTER NINE

ZANDER'S VOICE CRACKED through the silence like a whip and halfway up the stairs Mia froze. She turned to see him striding towards her with steely purpose and thrilling intensity. He took the stairs two at a time and stopped on the step one down from her and once she'd recovered from her shock she nearly passed out with excitement, because surely this could only mean one thing.

'You've realised I'm right,' she breathed, her heart leaping about her chest and shivers racing through her.

'I'm prepared to consider the possibility,' he said, his voice very rough, very low, smouldering energy pouring off him in great buffeting waves.

'What took you so long?'

'You've almost completely destroyed my brain's processing power.'

'What about your rule?'

'A temporary hiatus will do no harm.'

'You're going to break it for me,' she said giddily. 'And you were so adamant.'

'Don't overthink it,' he muttered, his gaze fixed to her mouth. 'I don't intend to.'

And she didn't want to. She didn't need to. How, or why, he'd changed his mind was none of her concern. She just wanted whatever came next.

'Here's to living in the moment.'

'I couldn't agree more.'

Eyes blazing, he grabbed her hand and before she could catch her breath he'd led her up the stairs and into his room. He kicked the door shut and pulled her into his arms and their mouths met in a desperate clash of heat and desire.

With a harsh groan that skated over her nerve-endings and set them on fire, Zander tightened his hold on her, exploring her mouth with such skill and intent that her limbs went weak. Lost to sensation, dizzy with his scent and revelling in the hard power of his body pressed up against hers, Mia wound her arms round his shoulders before her legs could give way and kissed him back with equal passion.

One large, warm hand found its way to the

back of her neck. The other moved to the base of her spine to clamp her in place. Eventually, the hot, wild, desperate kiss slid into ones that were slower, less feverish, but somehow all the hotter for it. She felt them everywhere, in her toes, in her fingers, even in her ears. The blood flowing through her veins heated and thickened. Her stomach liquefied.

With a soft moan, she twitched her hips so that his hardness pressed into the place where she so desperately ached for him. He slid the hand at the small of her back lower, over the curve of her bottom, and ground her against him, and that kicked everything up a gear.

The sparks of electricity that shot through her nearly took out her knees. Her heart began to pound even harder and desire poured through her like warm honey. She broke the kisses in order to gulp in some much-needed air and he took immediate advantage of the move by shifting his attention to her jaw, her ear, and then slowly, hotly, down her neck.

Instinctively, she dropped her head back to give him better access to wherever he wanted to go, her swollen, achy, tingling breasts desperate for his touch, but the high neckline of her dress was in the way and quite suddenly she needed both of them, her and him, naked, *now*.

Zander clearly shared her thoughts, or perhaps he sensed her urgency, because the devastating kisses stopped abruptly and his hands went from caressing to searching.

'Where's the zip on this thing?' he muttered after a moment of thorough searching that she hadn't minded one bit.

'At the side,' she said, her voice so thick and raspy she barely recognised it.

Having found the tab, he slowly slid it down and she shivered, though the room was warm. He reached down and slipped his hands beneath the hem at her knees to push her dress up, over her head and off.

His smouldering gaze roamed over her, taking in the black lace bra that these days barely contained her breasts and matching knickers. It lingered on her abdomen for a moment, and her heart fluttered, but she didn't want to think about the baby right now, about what this was and wasn't, so she stepped forwards, lost herself in the intensity of his expression and eased off his jacket.

'You're overdressed,' she murmured, her breath hitching as she unbuttoned his shirt and pushed that off him too and thought that God, she'd forgotten how magnificent his chest was. All those muscles. The solidity, the strength.

The night of his party, she hadn't had nearly enough time to fully explore the expanse of it or to properly savour the feel of his hair-roughened skin beneath her palms. Tonight, she planned to rectify that, so she put her hands on him and, emboldened by the shudder that ripped through him, slowly trailed her finger-tips over the ridges and dips. Her mouth watered at the thought of tasting him, and she leaned in closer, closer, shutting her eyes and breathing him in, but it seemed that he had other plans because he suddenly swept her up in his arms, carried her across the room and deposited her on the bed.

While she lay against the pile of pillows, catching her breath and recovering from the surprise move, Zander stripped off the rest of his clothes with impressive speed and efficiency and, although she'd seen it all before, it was as if she was looking at him for the first time.

She'd assumed her dreams had embellished his assets, but no. In the soft glowing light, she could see that his shoulders were just as broad as she remembered, his thighs just as powerful. And in between them, jutting up, long, thick and hard, the massive erection that had driven

her to heights of pleasure she'd never experienced before.

Her heart thudded wildly as he joined her
on the bed. He shifted onto his side, then half
rolled on top of her, and her entire body trem-
bled.

'Are you sure it's medically safe to do this?'
he said, smoothing back a rogue lock of hair
from her cheek.

'Definitely,' she said with a shiver at the unexpected nature of his touch. 'The doctor rec-
ommended leaving it for forty-eight hours, but
it's been longer than that so we're good.'

His dark eyes glinted. 'We are better than
good. We are exceptional.'

And Mia knew that he was an ace seducer,
that these smooth lines might be practised even
if some weren't, that making women swoon
was his thing, but nevertheless, she did exactly that. He lowered his head to hers, their
mouths meeting again for a slow, hot kiss that
sent flames flickering along her veins and dissolved her stomach, and her head actually spun.

Needing to touch him, she lifted her hands to
his shoulders and ran them over his hard muscles and into his hair, and he moved his beneath
her to unclip her bra. He tossed it aside and
then slid a hand from her waist up, and when

he cupped one breast with it, she moaned at the palpitations that jolted through her. She was so sensitive. She had goosebumps all over and quivered everywhere. His thumb brushed over her nipple and she almost came on the spot.

Had she felt this level of desperation before? she wondered with the one brain cell that was still functioning. She couldn't remember. She could barely recall her own name, especially when he replaced his hand with his mouth and she saw stars.

He lavished exquisite attention on her, taking his time, in no hurry to move on until, almost inside out with desire, she whimpered, 'I need more,' and he obligingly inched his way down her body, singeing her skin with his kisses, before finally stopping at the molten spot where she burned.

His hot, ragged breath on her made her quake with need. He removed her knickers, then put his hands on her knees and parted them. He draped her thighs over his shoulders and curled his arms around them. Then he put his mouth on her, where she so desperately throbbed for his touch and ached for his possession, and she had to bite her lip to stop herself from crying out, even though there was no one around to hear her except him.

Within seconds she was struggling for breath. He was going to blow the top of her head off. And soon. Her muscles were tightening and she was impossibly hot. Her heart was pounding. She was clutching at the sheet. The exquisite pleasure was building. A familiar tingling was beginning in her toes and then it was rolling up through her in a giant unstoppable wave until it tipped her over the edge, and she shattered.

Liquid heat rushed from her pelvis into every cell of her being. White lights flashed behind her eyes, while the contractions she felt vibrating through her went on and on, rendering her dazed and limp.

She gradually came to, to find Zander had moved and was once more gazing down at her from above.

'That was fast,' he said, his voice so low and rough it was almost feral.

Fast and intense and incredible. 'Hormones,' she said, still breathless, still dizzy. 'They've gone a bit mad.'

'This *is* going to be fun.'

A gleam lit the dark depths of his eyes and, incredibly, a fresh wave of desire washed over her. But she wanted to make him fall apart as she'd just done, for him to be putty in *her* hands, so she pushed him onto his back, arranged herself so she straddled him, and said, with a slow wicked smile, 'It certainly is.'

Zander woke late the following morning to an empty half of the bed, which would have been a cause for annoyance and alarm were it not for the mouth-watering smells that presumably came from the kitchen and meant that while Mia wasn't around to help him out with his mammoth erection she wasn't far away.

What a night, he thought with a yawn and a stretch. Her response to him had been as stunning as that first night they'd spent together. Over and over again she'd shattered in his arms, and she'd blown his mind more times than he could count. How his bed had survived it, he had no idea. Why he'd ever had reservations about sleeping with her again he couldn't imagine. What on earth had he been thinking? Together, like that, they truly were extraordinary.

After reassuring her that he'd *always* practised safe sex and that there hadn't been anyone since her anyway, for the first time in his life he hadn't used protection and it had been a revelation. She'd felt like warm, wet velvet and the heightened friction, the exquisite sensitivity and the unexpected intimacy had rocked his world.

Rubbing his eyes, Zander reached for his watch, which sat on the bedside table, and squinted at the dial. It was ten o'clock. And a Friday. He ought to have been at his desk over two hours ago, and under normal circumstances he would have been. Yet this morning, after that night, work didn't remotely appeal. What *did* appeal was firstly food and secondly returning Mia to his bed and keeping her there to explore further ways in which they could be exceptional.

He'd built up a very capable team in the six years since he'd taken over from Leo as CEO of Stanhope Kallis, he reminded himself as he tossed aside the covers. The three-hundred-year-old company, which employed thousands across the globe and had a several-billion-euro turnover, wouldn't collapse if he didn't go in today. Unable to find his shirt, he located his shorts and trousers and pulled them on. Then, lured by the distinctive scent of frying bacon, he headed downstairs.

Mia was at the stove with her back to him, humming along to the Christmassy sounding music emanating from her phone. No wonder he hadn't been able to find his shirt. She was wearing it. And not a lot else, it appeared.

For a moment, he leaned against the door frame and simply drank in the view. The long bare legs. The glimpses of her bottom which the tails of his shirt didn't quite cover. All that red-gold soft, silky hair. And as the seconds ticked by, he was filled with the clamouring urge to walk up to her, wrap his arms around her from behind, push her hair to one side and kiss her neck until she was breathless. Instead, because he did still possess *some* self-control and that somehow felt important, he pushed himself off the door frame and walked into the room.

'Good morning,' he said, thinking it was a very good morning indeed.

'Good morning,' she replied, looking charmingly sexy and dishevelled and disconcertingly at home at his stove.

Aware that what little self-control he'd prided himself on retaining was in danger of slipping away in response to the evident curve of her breasts and the hard points of her nipples beneath the crumpled white cotton, Zander slid his gaze to the pots and pans and food beyond her. 'You're cooking breakfast.'

'I am,' she said, casting her eyes over his

torso for one long, lingering moment before abruptly turning back to the stove and flipping the bacon with the deftness of someone who'd done it many times before. 'I've made pancakes and French toast. The tomatoes are under the grill and the sausages are keeping warm in the oven with everything else.'

For both their sakes, Zander gave her a deliberately wide berth as he walked around the island to the other side and pulled out a stool. 'You don't need to cook for me.'

'I know. But I enjoy it and we need to eat. Are you hungry?'

'Ravenous.'

'Grab a plate.'

'Where did all this come from?' he asked, waving a hand at the dishes on the counter and those she was removing from various appliances that before this morning had never been used.

'The food hall down the road. I was going to go shopping myself, but Tony insisted on taking my list and having everything delivered instead.'

'I'm not surprised he went out of his way to be helpful if you were dressed like that.'

'It was the first thing that came to hand and he was in an apologetic frame of mind.'

A dart of guilt stabbed him in the chest. Roping Tony in to ease his conscience while he'd been hiding out at the office hadn't been his finest moment, although he had done his best to make up for it in the bath he and Mia had taken some time around midnight. 'It looks better on you than it does on me.'

'I don't know about that,' she murmured, her gaze drifting over his chest once again, leaving fresh scorch marks in its wake. 'You could wear a paper bag and still look gorgeous. But if it makes you feel better, I threw on some leggings and a coat.'

That did make him feel marginally better. He didn't know why. Tony was sixty-five and happily married, with three children and ten grandchildren, and jealousy had never been his thing.

'You could have just ordered something in,' he said, choosing to ignore the unfathomable twist of his gut and reaching for a perfectly warm plate.

'You can't survive on restaurant food for ever.'

'I'm living proof you can.'

'Do you mind I took over your kitchen?'

After considering her question for a moment, Zander decided he did. He found both the sensual domesticity of the scene and the fact that he couldn't remember the last time anyone had cooked for him unnerving. But he couldn't tell her that. Only a few days ago he'd used it as bait to entice her to move in, so instead he gave her a smile that had been described as devastating on more than one occasion and said, 'Not at all.'

'I would have asked, but I didn't want to wake you.'

'That I wouldn't have minded either,' he said, dropping three rashers of bacon on his plate and thinking of all the very pleasurable and not at all domesticated ways in which she could have done so. 'Remember that next time.'

Her gaze dipped to his mouth and darkened, as if she was imagining kissing him, and her breath caught. 'So there *is* going to be a next time?'

Of course there was going to be a next time. His hunger for her hadn't abated one bit.

'Sooner than you might think if you keep looking at me like that,' he said, adding eggs, tomatoes and sausages to the bacon and noting the wild fluttering of the pulse at the base of her neck.

The faintest of smiles tugged at her lips. 'We can't have that after all the effort I've been to.'

'Then save the smouldering for later.'

'Would that be wise?'

'You're the one who pointed out the wisdom of it in the first place,' he said, needing her to see things his way because he didn't want to contemplate not having sex with her again. 'We've slept together on two separate occasions and, from my point of view, the world hasn't imploded. How's it looking from yours?'

'Still intact.'

That was a relief. And yet the tiny frown that appeared between her eyebrows was a concern. 'Are you having second thoughts?'

'No,' she said, 'but I am wondering how long we give it.'

He had no idea. He didn't have a template for this totally unprecedented situation. All he had was logic and the points she'd so effectively made last night. 'I suggest we continue until the attraction disappears and we can co-exist in peace.'

'What if it doesn't disappear?'

'It will,' he said, as much to assure himself as her. 'In my experience, which, as you know, is extensive, it always does. Generally after one night, admittedly, but even the longest lasting, most spectacular firework burns out eventually.'

Mia didn't look convinced as she took the seat opposite him and loaded her plate with

French toast and tomatoes. 'I'll have to take your word for it.'

'You do that. And while you're doing that, think of the fun we're going to have in the meantime. I know I am.'

Her breath caught and her cheeks flushed and for one electrifying moment he thought she was going to suggest abandoning breakfast after all. But a second later, disappointingly, she'd given herself a visible shake and pulled herself together. 'That can wait.'

Could it? That was a shame. Unless she'd somehow thought of a better plan. 'What do you have in mind instead?'

'Something I've been wanting to do for the last three days,' she said with an enticing stretch for some cutlery.

That did sound interesting. 'Which is?'

'Regardless of how you feel about relationships, it's looking increasingly likely that we're going to be having one of *some* kind. So I think we should get to know each other better. I'd like to find out more about the father of my child. We've already talked quite a bit about me. So, while we eat, I'd like to talk about you.'

CHAPTER TEN

OUTWARDLY, ZANDER SWALLOWED down the eggs he'd just put in his mouth and carefully returned his fork to his plate with barely a sound. Inwardly, however, all thoughts of fun had vanished, and alarm was now rushing into every millimetre of his body, coating his skin in a film of cold sweat and threatening a reappearance of the coffee he'd drunk.

Talk about himself?

He'd never heard a more preposterous, more petrifying proposal in his life. It went against his number one principle when it came to women—not getting personal and staying safe.

The exposure…

The vulnerability…

Even the thought of knowingly putting himself in such a position made his blood chill and his insides shrivel. Wasn't that yet another reason he'd stayed away from her this week? Because deep down he'd feared that all too soon small talk would not suffice.

Well, he'd been right.

He did not want to talk about himself. At all. But what choice did he have? Given the circumstances, Mia's suggestion wasn't outrageous and she wouldn't let him get away with suddenly remembering a meeting. If he stonewalled too much, she might start to wonder what his problem was. She might figure it had to be bad and decide she didn't want him around their baby. The likelihood of getting her to agree to marry him would become even more remote than it already was.

And even if that *didn't* happen, her point about them being connected for years to come was a salient one. He'd even told her the same thing at dinner the night she'd moved in, just before he'd offered her a slice of blueberry tart. In six months or so, all being well, they'd be bringing up a child. Together. Which would presumably require communication of some sort on a regular basis.

So perhaps he ought to practise. He didn't have to reveal anything particularly deep. Much of his life was already in the public domain. He had decades of experience in deflection and obfuscation, when it came to others as well as himself. But on a superficial level he could give her elements of what she wanted, surely. If he prevaricated, she'd only push harder and with his inexperience he'd likely lose control of the narrative, which was not an appealing prospect.

So he cleared his throat, sat back and braced himself. 'What do you want to know?' he said, ignoring the sliver of unease and deliberately relaxing his shoulders, as if this conversation really was no big deal.

Mia took a sip of orange juice, thought for a moment, then said, 'Do you like your life?'

Zander's eyebrows shot up. That was what she was opening with? Existentialism? He didn't know how he felt about his life. He didn't often analyse it. Or ever, in fact. So he went for a smouldering smile and a pleasingly ambiguous, 'Who wouldn't?'

'Well, a baby, I would imagine.'

'I see no reason for anything to change,' he said, largely because he hadn't been to a party in a fortnight and he hadn't slept with anyone other than her in the last six months, so it already had.

She frowned. 'So you're not planning on being that involved, then.'

He shot her a wolfish grin. 'I'm very good at multitasking, I think you'll agree.'

LUCY KING

155

'Because I need to know that if anything happens to me, you'll be there.'

Ah. The grin slid from his face and he shifted on his seat. 'What do you think is going to happen to you?' he said, his gut clenching in the oddest way at the idea of anything happening to her at all.

'Probably nothing. I mean, I don't carry the gene that caused my mother's disease, so that's not a worry, but there is only me. And I don't ever want a child of mine to face the prospect of growing up alone.'

'I'll always be there,' he said, for once deadly serious. 'And if for some reason I'm not, I have a lot of siblings and in-laws. Whatever happens, our child will never be alone. You have my word.'

'Do you trust them?'

'Yes.'

'Do you get on well with them?'

'Sure.'

At least, he didn't get on *badly* with them. En masse, they could be a challenge, what with the instinctive, natural way they interacted, which confounded and unnerved him in equal measure. He found the marriages unfathomable and he'd never get used to the displays of affection between those who'd coupled up, which was why he'd be avoiding the annual Christmas get-together this evening. But on a one-to-one basis they were easier. Under those circumstances he got on with each of them in different ways.

'So why don't you have any photos of them?'

Why on earth would he? If he had photos of them then they'd want ones of him and that wasn't happening when who knew what could be captured in an unguarded moment. 'I'm not one for photos.'

'If I were you, I'd have albums of the things. I so envy you your siblings,' she said with a sigh. 'I used to imagine I had four. Two older, two younger. Two boys, two girls. We'd get up to all sorts of things. Japes and escapades and jam sandwiches. We never argued. It was always perfect. Too much Enid Blyton from the library, probably. And then something would happen to burst the bubble and I'd land back in reality, which was pretty bloody awful most of the time and somehow even worse after one of my idyllic daydreams.'

'At least you had a mother who loved you,' he said, not much liking the shadows that clouded the clear blue of her irises, which set off an odd twang in his chest.

'Didn't yours?'

'The only person my mother truly loves is

herself. She isn't, and never has been, around all that much.'

'Not even when you were young?'

'Especially not then.'

'What about your father?'

'He had a fatal heart attack eighteen years ago,' he said. 'He was the stiff upper lip type. Aristocratic, stern and obsessed with building an empire. He didn't have much time for us either. Or rather, none of us but Leo, who he was grooming to inherit the company.'

'That must have hurt.'

He gave a shrug, as if it hadn't cut him to the bone before he'd decided to deal with it by simply shutting his emotions down. 'I didn't know any differently.'

'So what was growing up with but without them like?'

Pretty bloody awful, to steal her phrase, but this conversation had turned out to be deeper than he'd anticipated. It was one thing her voicing her fears, but he couldn't afford to do the same. He wouldn't even know how. In his desire to erase the wistfulness from her expression he'd already revealed too much and he really didn't need the sympathy that was radiating in his direction.

'It was fine,' he said with a dismissive wave of his hand. 'We had excellent nannies.'

'That's no substitute.'

'We survived.' He shot her his wickedest smile. 'Some of them were stunning.'

'Of course they were,' she said dryly. 'I hope I get a chance to meet them.'

'Who?' Not the nannies, surely.

'Your brothers and sisters.'

Well, *that* was never going to happen. He hadn't introduced anyone to his family since Valentina, who'd convinced him such a thing was normal and whom he'd been trying to please, and what a waste of time that had turned out to be.

These days, his conquests were never around long enough to even enquire into his family and none of them, before Mia, had ever meant anything anyway. Not that she meant something, of course. It was just…well, he didn't know what it was.

But as his pulse slowed and his lungs began to function again, it occurred to him that he'd have to explain her and the pregnancy to his siblings at some point, preferably before the press got wind of it, so why not at the party this evening? He'd declined the invitation, not needing the peculiar tension and roiling stomach that meeting up with them always provoked in him, but that was easily fixable. He could handle any tricky questions that came his way. He'd simply smile lazily and bat them away as he usually did. The addition of Mia to the proceedings would certainly be novel.

'If you're feeling up to it,' he said, stuffing the unacceptably stirring emotions back into the locked box where they belonged, 'you can meet some of them tonight.'

The Stanhope family's dinner was being held in a small private room at an exclusive central London members' club that was housed in a building which dated back to 1774.

Climbing the sweeping marble staircase with Zander at her side, Mia was glad she'd had the opportunity earlier to pick up a suitable outfit from her flat. As unassuming as the exterior of the club was, it was not the sort of establishment that would look favourably on the comfy jeans and baggy sweatshirts she'd packed for her stay with him. Nor did she want to wear her black dress and feel like one of the staff. More importantly, however, there was no way she was going to meet members of his ultra-glamorous family in anything other than her best cocktail dress and highest heels.

She could scarcely believe she was here in the first place, if she was being honest. She'd only suggested meeting them because her curiosity over his upbringing had got the better of her. How could his childhood possibly have been fine when it sounded as if he and his siblings had largely been neglected by the two people who should have done the opposite? What effect would that have on a boy, and the man he'd become?

At least *she'd* had eleven years of love and affection and a photo to prove it. Even though she couldn't remember much about that period of her life, eclipsed as it had been by time and the illness that had destroyed her mother and robbed her of her adolescence, she knew she'd been adored and nurtured in the beginning, that there had been shared hopes and dreams, and there was comfort in that.

'Are you all right? You're very quiet.'

Zander's murmured concern cut into her musings about how he was so much more complex than she could ever have imagined, and she switched her attention to the evening ahead.

'Just nervous.'

'Don't be.'

'That's easy for you to say,' she said as up and round they went, her stomach fluttering more wildly with every step she took. 'They're your relatives. You've known them all your life. Do they know about me?'

'They're about to.'

'Are you planning on telling them about the baby?'

'It would be the ideal opportunity. Would you mind?'

'I don't know,' she confessed with a faint frown. 'What if they hate me? What if they think I'm a gold-digger who's deliberately trapped you or something?'

'They won't,' he said, glancing across at her, clearly bemused. 'Why would they?'

'I don't know that either. I've never done anything like this before.' She took a deep breath and let it out slowly, but it didn't do much to ease her jitters. 'I can't believe I thought it was a good idea.'

'You've never done this before?' he asked, one dark eyebrow arched in surprise.

'I'm not very good at relationships. I've only had three and none of them reached the meet-the-family stage. Not that that's what this is exactly, I know.'

'What about the fairy tale?'

'It's remained elusive.'

'Why?'

'I've been told I have a tendency to cling,' she said with a wince. 'It's a fair assessment. I so badly want to be part of something bigger than just me, it sometimes skews my judgement.'

'That's understandable.'

Now the surprise was all hers. 'Is it?'

'Given your upbringing, I would say so.'

'That's quite some insight.'

'It's logic, nothing more.'

She supposed it was. It didn't require a degree in psychology to look at the past to see how it influenced the present. She'd spent so many hours doing precisely that she was practically an expert.

'Would it be logical to assume this is a first for you, too?' she said.

'Why would you assume that?'

'Because presumably the women you sleep with—just the once, naturally—would get even more of the wrong idea if they were introduced to your family.'

'Now *that's* insight,' he said, neither confirming nor denying her point, which she would have found interesting had she not been reminding herself that *she* wouldn't be making that mistake, of course.

There was nothing to read into this evening, so she would *not* be thinking about how if she did marry him she'd be instantly part of the something bigger she'd always longed for. The in-laws. The nieces and nephews. The birthdays, the Christmases, the belonging.

She was only here because she was carrying his child. None of it was real and there was no point in wishing it was. Which she didn't. Because that would be a one-way ride to despair, as she'd reminded herself this morning while she'd lain beside him, staring up at the ceiling in the half-light, wondering where they went from there.

Did they view last night as a one-off and hope it had done the trick? she'd asked herself, the questions tumbling around in her head like clothes in the wash. Or did they carry on indulging the off-the-charts chemistry and cross their fingers that it wouldn't cause problems down the line? Neither course of action had seemed like a solid one but with desire stirring and thoughts of waking him up *extremely* nicely to be checked, option two had felt infinitely preferable.

As long as she heeded her own advice and kept in mind that what existed between them was purely physical, she'd assured herself, her heart would be safe. That he hadn't slept with anyone else since her was irrelevant and didn't require analysis, even if it had come as a surprise. Chemistry was simply one set of pheromones responding to another. She wouldn't fall in love with him because fundamentally they wanted different things, so he was not and never would be the man of her dreams, and she wouldn't be marrying him anyway.

'This way,' he said when they reached the landing. 'Showtime.'

Zander planted a hand on her back to propel her in the direction of a purple panelled door. Banking the nerves and resisting the urge to cling to him for support, Mia braced herself for a situation that was filled with the unknown and went on in.

Great swathes of raspberry-coloured velvet hung at the multi-paned sash windows. The walls were lined with striped silk of a similar but paler hue and the woodwork was painted a fresh light green. The comfortable furnishings and abstract art were a clever combination of modern and traditional. With elaborate cornicing, gilt moulding and tassels dangling from the spectacular chandelier, sumptuous the room was, minimalist it was not.

But, beyond that, she barely noticed the décor. The warm pressure of his hand on her back vanished. All she saw was a bunch of impossibly beautiful, achingly sophisticated people, chattering animatedly in both Greek and English, clearly at ease and enjoying themselves, and all she felt now was a wave of longing so strong it nearly took out her knees.

'Zan!' said a stunning brunette, catching sight of them and heading over, her smile so bright it was blinding. 'What are you doing here? We didn't think you were coming.'

She reached up and planted a kiss on Zander's cheek, and while he returned it Mia grappled for control because she had to remember that this family was not and never would be hers.

'Change of plan.'

'And with a *date*,' said the woman, her brown eyes sparkling as they took in Mia with rampant curiosity. 'It has to have been *years* since that last happened. What was her name?' She appeared to think for a moment and then said, 'Aha! Valentina. That was it, wasn't it?'

At her side, Mia felt Zander tense but his smile stayed in place and he continued to radiate nonchalance, which was a *very* interesting paradox.

'I don't recall,' he said languidly while Mia thought, not so languidly, Valentina? Who was *she*? 'Mia, this is my sister, Thalia. Thalia, this is Mia Halliday.'

Thalia held out her hand. 'It's a pleasure to meet you.'

Parking the intriguing Valentina for now, Mia shook it and returned his sister's mega-watt smile with an attempt at one of her own. 'Likewise.'

'Great dress.'

'Thank you.'

Zander had certainly approved of it, she recalled, a hot flush rolling through her body from her feet up. Earlier this evening, she'd emerged from her bedroom in the gold fringed knee-length affair that she liked because it was easy to wear and shimmied when she moved, only to be hustled straight back into it. 'Liquid sunshine' was how he'd described it, while whipping it off her before tumbling her to the bed, messing up her hair and make-up and making them very late indeed.

'You look familiar,' said Thalia with an assessing tilt of her head and a slight frown. 'Have we met before?'

'I catered Zander's birthday party back in October,' said Mia, batting away the steamy memories of earlier in order to be able to concentrate on the conversation happening now. 'You may have seen me there.'

'Ah, yes, that's right. I remember. Zander was scowling at you.'

'I was not.'

'My mistake,' his sister said, a recognisably wicked glint dancing in her eyes. 'If I recall correctly, it was the risotto that was the source of your displeasure.'

Oh? 'The risotto?' said Mia, her eyes narrowing as she slid her gaze in his direction. 'What was wrong with it?'

'Nothing,' he said, sounding supremely unperturbed but looking as though he'd quite like to throttle his sister.

Thalia was evidently unaware of the danger she was in. 'He thought the flavours unoriginal,' she said blithely. 'Which they were very much not.'

Unoriginal? Seriously? 'Did you?'

With a tut of exasperation, he leaned in close and bent his head. 'I wanted you,' he murmured, the admission for her ears only. 'You didn't want me. It was frustrating. But I wasn't going to tell Thalia that. She'd never have let it go. Your risotto was perfect.'

'Oh,' she breathed softly, her pique melting clean away. 'Well, that's all right then.'

'I'll make it up to you later.'

Why later? she thought giddily. She wanted him to make it up to her now. Because in response to his proximity, his warm breath that caressed her skin, the spicy scent that scrambled her senses, her pulse was drumming in her ears and even though they'd spent all day in bed, the desire that was sweeping through her was as fresh and hot and wild as ever. But, unfortunately, they were in public, so she got a grip and murmured, 'I'll hold you to that.'

'I'll make sure you do.'

Straightening slowly, almost reluctantly, she sensed, Zander cleared his throat, shoved his hands in his pocket and switched his attention back to his sister. 'Where's Santi?'

'Phone call,' said Thalia, fanning her face with her hand. 'He'll be back in a minute. So are you two an item?'

'When am I ever an item?'

'What's the deal, then? Because I nearly got singed just now—and don't take this the wrong way, Zan—but Mia isn't your usual type.'

'I know she isn't,' he said, enviably cool while Mia still burned. 'She is, however, pregnant, and the baby's mine.'

CHAPTER ELEVEN

WHY ZANDER HAD chosen that particular moment to impart their news, he had no idea. All he knew was that the words had bizarrely been piling up on his tongue from the moment they'd walked into the room and had spilled out before he could stop them.

Perhaps he'd been thrown by the unusual intensity of the unpleasantness that had slithered into the pit of his stomach in an all too familiar way on seeing his siblings chatting away with each other so naturally.

How did they do it? he'd wondered queasily as he'd watched his younger brother Atticus laugh at something Thalia had said. They were twins, so that had always given them a special bond, he assumed, but what excuse was there for Leo to instinctively lean into Willow, his wife, when she touched him lightly on the arm? More bafflingly, *why* did they do it? Didn't they care about exposing their emotions to each other and risk being destroyed? Didn't they realise how vulnerable they were making themselves?

These were questions he'd never been able to answer so, as usual, he'd buried them deep, profoundly relieved that he was so practised at hiding and dissembling that no one would have had the slightest idea what was going on, which meant that a far more likely explanation for blurting out that Mia was pregnant was that he'd been shaken to the core by his response to the heated moment they'd shared in the aftermath of Thalia's unforgivably good memory.

For several long, heart-thumping seconds it had felt to him as though they were the only two people in existence. Overwhelmed with excoriating need, he'd been a hair's breadth from kissing the life out of her in front of an audience, which had never been his thing, and he thanked God he'd come to his senses in time.

Either way, the news was now out, suspended in the ether, immobilising every animate thing. There was a stunned frozen silence, which lasted several thudding beats of his pulse and a full revolution of his stomach, then the room erupted into a flurry of excited activity.

'Congratulations,' said Leo, striding forwards, smiling broadly and clapping Zander on the back before introducing himself to Mia and kissing her warmly on both cheeks.

'Will you be getting married?' asked Atticus, to which Mia replied 'No' at the same time as Zander said 'Yes'.

Then it was the turn of Willow, an artist with piercings and multicoloured hair, who shouldn't have suited his tightly controlled older brother but somehow did. 'How are you feeling?' she said, addressing Mia, who was looking a little shellshocked by the hugs and kisses that were coming her way.

'Anything I can do to help,' added Zoe, another sister-in-law, Atticus' wife, mother of one, soon to be two, 'let me know.'

Zander accepted the congratulations automatically, waiting with his breath stuck in his throat for the incredulity, the doubts, the ribbing, because surely at least one of them would point out how unsuited to the role of father he was. But no one said anything. The subject of his perceived lifestyle—wholly incompatible with a baby, as Mia herself had pointed out— didn't come up once. Of his self-centredness and lack of depth, not a word. Instead, to his astonishment, Leo insisted on a toast, of all things.

When they sat down to eat, two glasses of champagne and five minutes later, Zander was still waiting on tenterhooks for the other shoe to drop but, staggeringly, it didn't. Conversation flowed from the children to the company to Daphne and Olympia—his two youngest sisters, who weren't in attendance—and then moved on to their mother.

'Have you heard the latest from Selene?' said Thalia as she helped herself to some potatoes.

On easier to understand ground now, but nevertheless thinking that couldn't possibly be it, Zander sat back and raised his eyebrows. 'No. Why? What's she been up to?'

'She's been arrested for cavorting topless on a beach. Not the done thing in the Maldives, apparently.'

'Just what I need when we're about to launch the new cruise line arm of the business,' he said dryly. 'Her timing is impeccable, as always.'

'Don't worry,' said Atticus, head of the company's legal department. 'I'm on it. Any damage will be limited.'

'You'd think a full-size nude portrait would be enough to satisfy even the most determined exhibitionist,' Leo mused, topping up Mia's water glass. 'Although I suppose that *was* six years ago.'

'I still haven't got over it,' Zander said with a wince and a shudder. 'Talk about mortifying.'

'Hey, that's one of the finest pieces of work I've ever produced,' protested Willow without rancour. 'It launched my career.'

'I went to one of your exhibitions,' said Mia, who up to that point had hardly said a word, which was odd when she was not usually backward in coming forward. 'In London. Three years ago. It was amazing. You're incredibly talented.'

Willow beamed. 'Thank you. I'd love to paint you if you're up for it. I know I'm hardly one to talk, but the colour of your hair is highly unusual. Your skin is incredible. You'd look great in pastels. What do you think?'

By the look of things, Mia didn't know what to think. Wide-eyed and pink-cheeked, she appeared to be struck dumb. She opened her mouth. Then closed it. When she did manage to formulate an answer, it was an unexpectedly tremulous, 'I don't know what to say.'

'Say yes,' prompted Willow.

Mia blinked. Then nodded. 'OK,' she said a fraction more firmly, with a small yet blinding smile. 'Yes.'

'Great! Maybe you could persuade Zander to pose too. That bone structure and that smile…

The delicious hint of wickedness... I've been trying to get him to sit for me for years, but to no avail.'

At the thought of it a shudder ran through him. 'I have a global multi-billion-euro company to run,' he said, hiding his recoil of horror behind an apologetic grin and a what-can-I-do? sort of a shrug. 'I hate to disappoint you, but my spare time is limited.'

'I'll make it happen one day.'

No, she wouldn't. Because Willow liked to get to know her subjects by delving deep. Apparently, it added a certain depth and luminosity to her work. But if she dug around in his psyche, she'd find nothing luminous, nothing good, and the sense of worthlessness that lurked inside him was *not* for public display.

'Don't hold your breath.'

To his relief, the conversation then moved on to other less troublesome topics, but for some reason he couldn't stop thinking about Mia's smile when she'd agreed to sit for his sister-in-law. Something about it had felt important. He couldn't put his finger on what.

As the evening progressed, he continued to ponder the conundrum as they ate and drank and he watched her from afar. At first she'd preferred to observe the proceedings rather than participate in them. But gradually she seemed to relax and the balance shifted in the other direction. Before long, she and his siblings were chatting away as if they'd known each other for years instead of hours.

He largely listened and learned. Atticus and Zoe had recently been to a restaurant that served its customers in the dark, which prompted a discussion about the importance of senses when dining and gimmickry. Santi was buying an island off the Brazilian coast. Mia's dream holiday destination was Lapland, to see the aurora borealis.

One part of him ached with envy over her ability to fit in so easily and tried desperately to work out how she was doing it. Another was dazzled by the way she somehow shone, in a way that had nothing to do with the sexy gold sparkly dress she had on.

A third, however, was noting that she was avidly drinking everything in, wholly wrapped up in the banter and the affection, and quite suddenly, just as coffee and chocolates were being served, he had an epiphany.

He knew exactly what he'd seen in that smile. Longing.

This was what she'd always dreamed of, he realised with a rush to the head, stunned that he hadn't figured it out sooner. To be part of a family. To belong. And while he would never be able to offer her the love she wanted when he abhorred emotion, especially of the sentimental kind, and simply wasn't capable of it anyway, it was within his power to give *this* to her.

Marriage was no longer as remote a possibility as it had felt last night, he thought with a surge of satisfaction. Securing his position in case, unlike his siblings, she recognised his lack of depth and selfishness and took against it and decided she'd had enough, was once again at the top of his agenda. Because now, after days of wondering what the hell he was going to do about it, he had the leverage to get it.

What an absolutely fascinating evening, Mia reflected, kicking off her shoes back at the apartment and padding after Zander into the kitchen. And to think she'd been so nervous. His announcement had come completely without warning, but she hadn't had time to panic over how all those beautiful people were going to take the news of her pregnancy because, to her utter amazement and relief, she'd been enveloped in warmth and any concerns she'd had had simply disappeared.

There'd been no sly comments, no judgement, just delight and support to an extent that she'd never have expected. She hadn't met any of them before—they moved in *very* different circles—but that hadn't dimmed their effusiveness or acceptance of her and their nephew-or niece-to-be one bit, and for a while she'd been so overwhelmed, her throat so tight, that she'd hardly been able to speak.

But at least she hadn't fallen into the trap of thinking any of it was real. Every time she *had* caught herself drifting off into dangerous little daydreams in which Zander was interested in her welfare for her sake and not just their baby's and they were all one big happy family, she remembered him telling Thalia—most emphatically—they were not an item and hauled herself back on track.

Instead, she'd eaten supper without really tasting it—a rarity—and observed the dynamics like a kid with their face pressed up against the window of a sweetshop, only allowing herself to be drawn into the conversation once she'd strengthened her defences.

And hadn't those dynamics been intriguing. Zander's exchange with Willow on the subject of his reluctance to sit for a portrait had been particularly interesting. She didn't buy his 'not enough time' excuse. Everyone else had managed to make time. Their portraits all hung in the exhibition she'd been to. But not his. Behind the smile and the careless shrug, she thought she'd caught a flicker of irritation in his eyes. And something else. Something that had looked a bit like fear. Which was odd, because while she could understand the irritation if he genuinely didn't want to be painted, what on earth would he have to fear?

And that wasn't the only perplexing aspect of the evening. Forget Valentina for a moment, whoever she might be. Of far greater interest had been the other undercurrents she'd sensed swirling around him. It had been clear that everyone there was very fond of him and that the dinner had been a happy, relaxed occasion, but for some reason he'd seemed on edge. Sort of removed from the proceedings. He hid it well, but once or twice she'd even caught him looking at his siblings as if they were a different species, which was bizarre.

And what was the lazy smile, the lounging and the insouciant drawl all about? That wasn't the real him. She'd glimpsed the man behind the mask and he was far more layered than he was making out. The conversation they'd had on the way up was an example of that. Yet the minute they'd walked in, it was as if he'd flicked a switch and become a completely different person and she didn't think it was a one-off because no one called him out on it.

Why did he feel the need to put on a show, especially for his nearest and dearest? What was going on beneath the handsome, laid-back and very assured surface? And if she asked, would he ever tell her?

Having furnished Mia with a cup of the green tea she favoured, Zander made himself the thick black coffee he preferred and then joined her at the breakfast bar end of the island. Now he knew how to get what he wanted, like any deal, he was keen to get it wrapped up. Before he got side-tracked by her dress, her tousled hair and sexily smudged eye make-up and the moment passed. So he pulled out a stool, sat down opposite her and gave her a level look. 'We need to talk.'

'We do indeed,' she agreed with an equally level look of her own. 'You can start by telling me why you were so on edge tonight when it was such a wonderful evening.'

He stilled. His pulse skipped a beat. What the hell?

'I wasn't on edge,' he said, his intentions for the conversation momentarily derailed.

'Not outwardly,' she conceded. 'Outwardly, you were all lazy smiles and devilish charm from the minute we walked into that room. But it felt like some sort of a front, because you seemed watchful and wary. There but not really there. As if you'd landed from another planet. I'd like to know why.'

Well, *that* wasn't happening. He could barely unravel it in his head, let alone articulate it. But how had Mia noticed? What had given him away? What else could she have seen?

He shifted on the stool and adjusted his jacket, his blood chilling at the thought of being so transparent. 'There's nothing to know.'

'I think there is.' She wrapped her hands around the cup and tilted her head, continuing before he could interject. 'I think that behind that gorgeous facade of yours there's a *maelstrom* going on. I mean, how could there not be? You have a mother who sounds as selfish and embarrassing as the tabloid press reports and a father who by your own admission was never around for you. That neglect has to have been painful beyond words. You don't seem at all comfortable around your siblings, and I find myself wondering if Valentina, whoever she is, is the reason you're so sceptical about love, if she's the one who made you feel vulnerable and exposed, out of control and powerless. For some reason I've yet to work out, the idea of sitting for your portrait terrifies you and right now a muscle is pounding in your cheek and your jaw is so tight it looks as if it's about to shatter. I'd like to know what you're feeling. What you're thinking. You never know, I might even be able to help.'

Zander didn't need help. He just needed this unnecessary psychoanalysis to stop, along with her terrifying perceptiveness. The expanding pressure in his chest was crushing the air from his lungs. A swarm of a thousand bees seemed to be buzzing in his head.

So much for dissembling. It was as if she'd drawn back the curtain to his soul and taken a good long look at it. How had she done that? Did she understand what she'd seen? How had he not noticed?

The situation was slipping dangerously out of hand. His very foundations were cracking and he couldn't allow that. He had to contain the emotions trying to break their bonds to surge through him. He had to restore order and regain control and remember why he'd wanted to talk to her in the first place. So he willed his head to clear and concentrated on his breathing until he was cold and numb and back in command of himself. 'That's quite some analysis.'

'You're a fascinating man and it was an illuminating evening.'

'Did you enjoy yourself?'

'Very much. Your siblings and their spouses are great. I can't think why you'd have a problem with them.'

And that was the way things were going to stay. With her not thinking about him. At least, not like that.

'Has it ever occurred to you that if you married me you'd have instant access to them?' he said. 'That you'd immediately become part of the something bigger you want?'

'It has,' she replied with a nod. 'Well, once. Briefly. On our way to the dinner. But we both know such a relationship would be built on sand.'

Did they? For his part, he wasn't sure he knew anything any more. 'What makes you say that?'

'It would never be real. It would never truly give me what I want. What I think I deserve. Unless you're in love with me, of course. Then we might have a chance. Is that the case?'

His heart gave a great lurch. His entire body clenched, every single cell he comprised curling up like a pill bug, and the coffee in his stomach turned acidic. 'No.'

'Might it ever *be* the case?'

'Absolutely not.'

'Ouch,' she said with a wince that he hoped to God didn't mean she *wanted* it to be the case because he'd have no idea how to handle that. 'At least you're honest.'

'You should try it some time.'

Her eyes widened for a moment and then she frowned. 'What do you mean?'

'Admit there'd be advantages to being married to me.'

'Such as?'

'Firstly, your business. With one snap of my fingers—' he gave one snap of his fingers '—I could make Halliday Catering the number one catering company in the country. Even the world.'

'I think I'd rather do it on my own, thanks all the same.'

'And then there's the money,' he continued undeterred, because he was now in control of this conversation. 'Consider the costs of bringing up a child. Childcare. Education. Housing. Is a second floor flat really where you'd want to be lugging a pushchair? I could buy us a house with a garden tomorrow. Employ round-the-clock nannies. You'd never have to worry about money again. You could go back to work as soon as you liked. And if that doesn't sway you, think of the sex. I can't imagine getting bored with that any time soon. Can you?'

Her gaze dipped to his mouth and darkened. 'No.'

'Love is no guarantee of happiness,' he said, resisting the sudden blinding urge to lean over, take her face in his hands and kiss the daylights out of her because, for what had to be the first time ever for him, that wasn't important. 'I like you. I admire everything you've achieved. Lots of marriages are built on less. Think of the bigger picture. Think of the aunts and uncles our child would have on tap. The cousins to play with. The grandmother, although I admit that might not be such a draw. We'd be a family, a unit, and one that could even expand. You'd no longer be alone. You'd have all the things you've always wanted, except one. Wouldn't that be something?'

For a while Mia didn't say anything. She just sat there, barely moving, as if somehow winded. The seconds ticked by. He could practically see her working through what he'd said, and he waited, his breath stuck in his lungs, for her response, which came a moment later.

She gave herself a shake, cleared her throat and swallowed hard. 'I tell you what,' she said with a tiny jut of her chin. 'You address the points I just made and I'll promise to think about it. How does that sound?'

What? No. Out of the question. Why on earth would he lay out all his flaws for her inspection? He had been reckless on many occasions, but he wasn't completely out of his mind. And what did she think she was doing, turning the tables on him? Wasn't the leverage supposed to be his?

'That sounds like blackmail,' he said, flabbergasted.

'Call it what you like,' she said with unbelievable cool, 'but you're asking a lot of me. You're asking me to give up on a major dream of mine, a dream I've had for years. I've already conceded so much. I agreed to move in here temporarily. I took a step back from my business. I spent three days *resting*, which was the hardest thing I've done in a long time. What sacrifices have you made? None, as far as I can see. In what areas are *you* compromising? We each owe it to our child to be as baggage free as possible by the time he or she comes along. It's taken me years, but I've dealt with mine. Can you say the same for yours?'

Well, no. He couldn't. He was aware he had a lot but he'd never addressed any of it. He'd always preferred not to analyse his behaviour or the reasons for it, but to simply live with his issues, as if fearing a hornet's nest that he might not be able to withstand if he prodded it. So he'd never wondered how his past influenced his present in the way she clearly had. He'd never considered how it might affect his future.

And that had been fine when it had affected no one but himself, but he no longer existed in isolation, he realised with an unsettling jolt. Whether he liked it or not, he now had someone else in his life to consider. Mia. And, in approximately six months' time, a baby who would be dependent on him for years.

His days of thinking only about himself were over. If he wanted to be better than his own parents, he had to adapt. He had to at least *try* and become a more complete human being. Because his kid *did* deserve the best version of himself, however inadequate that might be.

Currently, he was not that. He didn't even know what that could look like, although it had to be better than the mess he was at the moment. So perhaps he did need Mia's help. As she'd said, she'd worked through her issues. Could she sort through his?

Even if she couldn't, she'd still have to hold
up her end of the bargain, and he didn't have
to strip himself bare by telling her *everything*.
Some things, such as his reasons for not wanting his portrait painted and the black hole of
emptiness that lurked inside him, would never
be up for dissection.

But others?

Why not?

It would mean discarding a lifetime of keeping a firm lid on the box that contained everything he didn't want to think about. It would
mean exposing to her certain parts of his bleak
inner self that had never seen the light of day.
But if it got him what he wanted, if it neutral-
ised the possibility of her disappearing with
their child when she realised he was damaged
beyond repair, it was a price worth paying.

CHAPTER TWELVE

MIA HAD NOT really expected Zander to accept the deal that she'd offered him even though it had felt slightly on the exploitative side, which should have felt like payback, but annoyingly didn't.

In fact, when he *did*, she thought she must have misheard. That wouldn't have been beyond the realms of possibility. She'd been thoroughly distracted by the picture of marriage he'd painted, the silver-tongued devil. She'd been pondering the odd reaction she'd had to his declaration that he would never love her, which was nothing new and should not have come as a blow but had nevertheless caught her off-guard.

But she had to park all that for now. The glimpses of the man beneath the surface that she'd previously had had been accidental, she was certain. Tonight, he'd decided to actively seek her input—he must *really* want her to marry him, although she couldn't see why when surely he'd realised by now that he could trust her, her quick trip to the gallery notwithstanding—and it somehow felt momentous.

He took his time pouring himself the drink he'd muttered he'd need if he was really going to do this. More to deliberate where they should sit, before settling on the library downstairs, a cosy space that had two chairs, both facing a built-in electric fireplace, which meant there was no facing each other.

Mia sat in her chair and sipped her tea, tracking Zander's movements as he set the bottle he'd brought with him down in anticipation of a challenging conversation, he'd said, and sat in the chair next to her. The suspense was killing her, but she would not revert to old bad habits and push. She would sit back and let this play out in its own time. He would start when he was comfortable. To her relief, however, because patience really wasn't her strong point unless she was in the kitchen, she didn't have long to wait.

'So about this evening,' he said eventually, staring into the fire. 'I *was* tense.'

Aha. She knew it. 'Why?'

'I always am when we meet up as a group.'

He scowled and knocked back half of his drink. 'I just don't get them. They seem so relaxed with each other. I can't understand how they do it.'

So he *did* feel like an outsider. 'Well, obviously I have no experience of siblings,' she said, reminding herself to rein in her rampant curiosity and tread carefully, 'but I wouldn't have thought it's a conscious thing. Presumably, you spent your childhood together. You must all know each other inside and out. They're relaxed with you too.'

'Only because I make it easy for them.'

That wasn't necessarily true. 'I think you're underestimating yourself. By taking me along to dinner this evening and dropping our baby bombshell you could have made things very difficult for them indeed if they hadn't approved.'

'Possibly.'

Definitely. 'What do you think would happen if you dropped the facade?'

'I'm not sure I ever want to find out,' he said with a shudder that suggested she'd been right about the maelstrom.

'What are you hiding?'

'Nothing in particular.'

She found that hard to believe. At the very

least, his super confident exterior had to conceal a chronic lack of self-esteem. She should know. She'd suffered from it herself, and the fundamentals of their circumstances weren't that dissimilar.

'I'm just no good at relationships and I'd like to correct that,' he said gruffly. 'The last thing I want is to turn out like either of my parents.'

'You won't. I won't let you.' And besides, despite the occasionally odd way of showing it, he did have the baby's best interests at heart.

'I might if I don't figure out how to be better.'

'You run one of the largest private companies in the world,' she pointed out. 'You couldn't do that without building and maintaining relationships.'

He frowned and fell silent for a moment, as if he'd never considered that before. 'That's different,' he said eventually. 'That's work.'

'So it's just close personal ones you struggle with.'

'Yes.'

'Then what about Valentina? You must have dated her more than once. You introduced her to your family. You broke your rule for her.'

'Valentina predated the rule,' he said with a grimace. 'She was the reason for the rule.'

Oh? 'In what way?'

'We met at a party when I was nineteen and went out for six months. To begin with everything was great. But then she wanted more.'

'That's not entirely unreasonable.'

'I know.' He drained his glass and refilled it. 'So I tried to make it work. I *wanted* to make it work. As you said, I even introduced her to my family. But that wasn't enough. Apparently, I was unable to give her what she needed. I couldn't commit to her—' he winced '—emotionally.'

'Was that true?'

'I'm not very good at connecting on a deep personal level,' he admitted, sounding as though he was having to grind out every word.

'Or maybe you just weren't as into her as she was to you.'

'I was. Or at least I wanted to be. But it didn't end well. I didn't understand what I'd done wrong. She made her disappointment in me very clear. I've been careful to avoid a similar situation ever since.'

'That's understandable,' Mia said, intensely disliking this woman whom she'd never met. 'Who'd want to go through that again? Although it *was* sixteen years ago, which is a long time to let something like that dictate your sex life.'

'I don't deny I also like variety,' he said with a faint quirk of his lips.

Hmm. 'Yes, well, it seems to me that your so-called inability to connect on a deeper level isn't all that hard to figure out.'

'Isn't it?' he asked, shooting her a curious glance before returning it to the fire.

'With parents like yours, who by the sounds of things were never around much and therefore didn't engage with you when you were young, how could you ever have learned how to do anything else? Where were your role models?'

'I suppose I didn't really have any,' he conceded after a beat.

'Who supported you? Championed you? Listened to your worries?'

'I dealt with everything on my own.'

As she had done. She'd had no support, no one to celebrate her successes or go to with her worries either, and for years she'd questioned her value.

For her, catering college had turned that around. Surrounded by like-minded people, being kept busy doing something she loved, even though she'd been grieving for the mother she'd lost, she'd slowly made friends and under the guidance of mentors had discovered her sense of self-worth. It had given her the courage to believe in herself and to set up on her own and had got her through some tough times in the beginning.

But who had he had? No one.

'You were neglected,' she said, feeling a sudden hot rush of anger on his behalf, there and gone in a flash. 'You had no one to meet your emotional needs.'

He considered that for a moment then said with a nod, 'I suspect you're right.'

'How on earth did you handle it?'

'I learned not to let it affect me. Like you, there was nothing I could do to change it. I just had to accept it.'

'There's a world of difference between accepting a situation that was nobody's fault and one that was.'

'It's worked for me so far.'

'But it doesn't sound as though it's working for you now and I'm not sure what good leaving these things unaddressed has ever done anyone. So, having said all that, I do believe you can *learn* to connect with other people on an emotional level.'

'Can you?'

'Absolutely,' she confirmed with a nod. 'I'm an example of that. I didn't get what I needed from my parents either. Or, rather, I did, from one of them, but not for long. With no one around to validate your feelings and experiences you find yourself questioning your self-worth. Your self-esteem nosedives. You get used to doing everything on your own. You become so strong that any hint of vulnerability or any request for help feels like weakness. It's hard to let people in. But you have to at some point, because no one is an island. Life is so much better with other people in it.'

'I know that,' he said. 'Deep down, I've always wanted that. I've just never known how to do it.'

Her heart gave a little ache at that but she would not let it distract her. 'I'm not saying it doesn't take time because it does. And it's not easy either. But you can't move forward if you don't understand and make peace with the past. And you can't overcome your faults and your flaws if you don't acknowledge them in the first place.'

Mia finished and took a sip of her tea while that sank in.

'Do you want to know what my greatest flaw is?' he said after a moment, setting down his still full glass and turning to face her, his eyes dark and intent on hers.

Her heart skipped a beat. She wanted to

know everything there was to know about the gorgeous, brave, compelling man her child was lucky to have as its father, whatever his faults. 'Sure.'

'Not being able to control my need for you.'

And, as he reached for her, it was clear that Zander was done with this conversation, which filled Mia with as much disappointment as desire.

Zander had had to bring the conversation to a halt that night in the library. He'd been hit by one earth-shattering revelation after another and his bruised and battered brain simply hadn't been able to take any more. He'd had to take refuge in sex. By that point it was all he'd understood.

He hadn't liked Mia's point about his experience with Valentina overshadowing the last sixteen years. Her spin on it made him sound weak. Nor had he appreciated her implication that his so-called inability to connect on a deeper level was all in his head. It wasn't. It was a very real, very deep-rooted part of him. But at least she hadn't pushed him on what he was hiding. At least she hadn't had a chance to quiz him on why he would never sit for his portrait.

The rest of their conversation, though, which

had shone a spotlight on his upbringing, had made a whole lot of sense. Of course he'd been neglected. Of course he'd never learned how to communicate properly. He *hadn't* had anyone to observe and emulate. The nannies had been great, but they hadn't exactly set an example to follow. So how could he ever have known what to do?

And as for his siblings' ability to forge and maintain relationships, which had always bothered him because, after all, they'd all grown up in the same house, it occurred to him as he lay awake in the early hours of Saturday morning, the conversation looping around his head, that emotional neglect and having self-absorbed parents might affect different people in different ways. He'd overeaten. Leo had crashed a boat. Olympia had spent a year in rehab. Atticus and Thalia were twins, they'd had each other, which presumably had made things easier. And Daphne had certainly suffered. She'd been diagnosed with acute myeloid leukaemia at the age of thirteen and although she'd been in remission for nearly a decade, she'd spent most of her adolescence in and out of hospital. How had she coped with their parents' approach to parenting?

Discovering and accepting that his problem

with close personal relationships wasn't his fault, but rather a by-product of his less than ideal upbringing, was something of a game changer. It suggested he had no fundamental flaws, as he'd feared, and that he might not be as worthless as he'd always assumed, courtesy of the belief that if even his own parents weren't interested in him then it had to mean that there was nothing about him to be interested in.

Over the next forty-eight hours, the bleak emptiness that had existed inside him for so long like a living, breathing thing seemed to ease. Far from feeling raw and exposed in the aftermath of their conversation, as he'd expected, he was aware of an odd sense of lightness and liberation.

He found he wasn't even that bothered about pushing Mia to comply with her side of their deal any more. Marriage was no longer the pressing necessity it once had been. She'd seen into the deepest parts of him and hadn't run a mile. And why would she? Apparently, there wasn't anything there to run a mile from. So she had no reason whatsoever to deny him access to their child.

In fact, he was now really rather relieved she'd resisted. Marriage for the sake of their child would only have complicated the situation. They could easily co-parent apart. Many thousands of other people did.

He had further work to do on his journey to becoming a fully functioning human being, of course. The thought of large family gatherings was still going to make him uncomfortable for a while. He obviously had *some* flaws.

But he'd taken those first tentative steps and they hadn't been a disaster, and he was keen to take more because building a sustainable relationship with Mia and their child didn't now feel as impossible as it once had. The more he'd talked to her and shared with her, the more he'd learned and the less insurmountable the challenges he faced seemed.

She even had the ability to soothe his agitation on the rare occasion it arose. This morning, for example, he'd run his hand down her body and when he'd felt the very faint curve of her abdomen he, a man of thirty-five who'd stared down countless rivals in the boardroom and possessed more power and influence than the leaders of some small countries, had started to shake.

'Are you all right?' she'd murmured, but he hadn't been able to reply because he hadn't been all right at all. His pulse had been racing and the walls had been closing in on him and he'd genuinely thought he'd been going to faint even though he'd been horizontal at the time.

But then she'd put her hand over his and the dizziness had faded enough for him to start breathing in and out, deeply and slowly, to be able to push down hard on everything that was demanding to be let in until it had all gone away.

'I'm fine.'

'I know you have concerns about your ability to be a father,' she'd then said, 'but you *will* be good at it. You're instinctively protective, you want the best and you care. That's quite a start.'

Was that really what she thought of him? he'd wondered as the chaos raging inside calmed. Did she genuinely believe he'd succeed at this? Astonishingly, it had sounded as though she did.

'Well, when you put it like that,' he'd said, the doubt beginning to slink off in the face of her certainty, 'maybe it is.'

Attempting a deeper, more personal connection between them was nothing to fear, nothing to avoid. It might even be something to look forward to. Contrary to what he'd been led to believe, he wasn't a disappointment. He didn't lack depth or value. He was fine. And that he now knew it was all down to Mia who, if ca-

tering didn't work out, could retrain as a psy-
chotherapist. Whose insight and self-awareness
were to be envied. Who'd told him how much
she'd admired the way he'd thrown himself into
something he'd clearly found a challenge and
made him feel ten feet tall.

She hadn't given up on him. She'd fixed him.
Or some parts at least. And for that she de-
served a thank you.

Mia had never received much in the way of
presents. Her mother had left school to have
her and had then got a job as a part-time shop
assistant when Mia had started at nursery, but
there'd been little money for toys. And then,
later on, she hadn't had anyone to exchange
them with anyway.

So when Zander had told her he was giving
her an early Christmas present, once she'd got
over the urge to dance around the room and
smother him in kisses—a ridiculous overreaction—she hadn't been able to think what that
might be. A diamond necklace? Something for
the baby? A brand-new spatula? She hadn't a
clue.

Never in a million years would she have
imagined being driven to her flat first thing
on Monday morning to pack a bag of warm

clothes and find her passport. Less still could she have envisaged him then whisking her to the airport, where his private jet was sitting on the tarmac, sleek and white and sparkling in the frosty December sunshine.

'Where are we going?' she said in something of a daze as she handed her bag to a member of the crew and then walked with him towards the plane.

Zander grinned, clearly extremely pleased with himself, which for some reason made her head spin and her heart melt like a snowflake in the sun. 'It's a surprise.'

That was a phrase no planner of anything ever liked to hear.

'I'm not sure I like surprises.'

'You'll like this one.'

'How enigmatic.'

'Not any more,' he said, taking her hand as they went up the steps. 'Thanks to you, I'm an open book.'

Burning up with curiosity and nervous excitement, Mia entered the cabin ahead of him and thought that he certainly was that. He'd confessed that he'd shut the conversation down that night in the library because it had been too much to handle, but they'd talked a lot over the weekend. They'd compared childhoods. Shared stories and experiences. Discussed such wide-ranging topics as politics, books and culinary loves and hates. She'd wanted to discover as much as she could about the father of her child and she'd done exactly that.

Of the future there'd been less discussion but there was plenty of time. They had months. The important thing was that they were communicating, on a number of different levels, and things were looking rosy.

Her book, however, was slightly less open, of course. But if he knew that she was not only thinking about his marriage proposal but actually considering it, *in his favour*, he'd be unbearable. She could hardly believe she was entertaining the idea of it herself. She'd always been so resolute about only marrying for love, so convinced that that would give her everything she'd ever wanted.

But over the weekend she'd begun to wonder, would it?

What if she never fell in love? Or what if she did and it all went wrong? Could Zander be right? Was what they already had enough? She found him fascinating. They got on well. They were on the same parenting page, trusted each other enough to reveal the bad as well as the good, and the chemistry showed no signs of diminishing.

Dare she imagine that, given the fact that he'd changed his mind about opening up to her, albeit under duress, his opinion on other things might shift too? Like love?

She probably shouldn't, but she did nonetheless. Because evidently he hadn't always been against it. Surely his relationship with Valentina was proof of that. It had been short and he'd been young, but despite Mia's suggestion at the time that perhaps he hadn't been as into it as Valentina had been, in hindsight, he must have loved her for their breakup to have had such a long-lasting effect. And if he'd been capable of it once, perhaps, if he could get over the breakup, he could be so again, in theory, which did possibly throw a different light on the future.

'How long will we be away for?' she said, sitting down in one of the cream leather seats and fastening her seatbelt as she cast a glance over the matching sofas, the thick shortbread-coloured carpet and the polished walnut trim, more akin to a sitting room than an aircraft.

'One night only, so there's no need to panic. We'll be back by tomorrow afternoon.'

He knew her and her need to be near her
business too well.

'And the flight time?'

'Three and a half hours.'

Perhaps the destination was Athens. That
would be great. She would love to see where
he grew up. She might even get to meet his
mother, who, following her brush with the Mal-
divian law, had returned home and was under
strict orders not to leave it. But there didn't
seem much point in asking because she doubted
he'd tell her.

'However are we going to occupy ourselves?'

'There's a cabin at the back with a bed in
it,' he said as he took the seat opposite her and
smouldered. 'I'm sure we'll think of something.'

After take-off, they had breakfast. Over a
plate of pastries, she told him that she used to
dream her father was a pilot—or maybe a sci-
entist or a farmer—and create whole worlds
around him. She told him that, along with the
cooking, being able to lose herself in her imagi-
nation had come in handy when things had got
a bit much later on and she'd needed a way to
handle the resentment and anger that developed
along with everything else. He downed coffee after coffee and responded by confessing

that he'd dealt with the neglect he'd suffered by comfort eating, in a classically futile attempt to make himself feel better, which was why he was so disciplined in hitting the gym.

That reminded Mia of his muscles, as if she needed a reminder, and they headed to the cabin, where she joined the mile high club and for a deliciously long while stopped tormenting herself with the pros and cons of marrying him and didn't think about the possible engagement of her heart in all this.

She didn't notice that outside the sun was starboard or that the sky was darkening instead of brightening even though it was mid-morning. She was aware of nothing but the wild, all-consuming heat that burned between them and losing control of her body and mind.

It was only when they touched down, some three hours and several orgasms later, that Zander finally lifted his head from the crook of her neck and said with a grin that suggested he was thoroughly proud of himself, and not just because he'd repeatedly dissolved her bones, 'Welcome to Lapland.'

CHAPTER THIRTEEN

MIA DID NOT react to his announcement that they'd arrived in Lapland the way Zander had expected. He'd imagined a gasp of surprise and then perhaps a squeal of enthusiastic delight and a pleasing display of gratitude. He'd been so proud of himself that he'd thought of this. He'd never been any good at giving presents. He'd always worried about getting it wrong, as his parents invariably had on the rare occasion they'd remembered a birthday, and figured it would be simpler just to not give anyone anything at all.

But this had felt like a winner. Utterly fail-safe. Lapland was Mia's dream holiday destination. December was an excellent time of year to see the Northern Lights. She'd be thrilled, he'd assured himself as he'd fleshed out the plan and instructed his team of assistants to see to the details. He certainly was. What he was doing was the ultimate proof that he was complete and could operate in the relationship arena just as successfully as everyone else did.

But Mia wasn't thrilled. Her gasp was a sharp one of dismay rather than a breathy one of excited surprise. She wriggled out from beneath him and pulled on her clothes, pale and shaking, so quiet and withdrawn suddenly it was as if someone had switched her off. Shockingly cold after all that heat, buffeted by confusion, Zander was too stunned to do anything but go through the motions as they disembarked the plane and went through Customs.

Now, they were in the car for the twenty-minute journey that would take them to the treehouse cabin where they were to be spending the night. Mia sat turned away from him, staring out of the window, but he could tell she was battling tears—*tears*—and his shock gave way to a surge of emotion that he just couldn't contain.

Why was she so upset? was the question that pounded through his head while he flailed about for an explanation, completely at sea and devastated, the pride, the hope, the relief draining utterly away. Had he got it wrong? How? It didn't seem possible. But he must have done. Why else would she be crying?

Theos, he was *no* good at this. Communication. Relationships. Trying to do something that he thought might make someone else happy. He never had been. Why he'd ever believed he'd be able to change the habits of a lifetime he had no idea. As if one weekend of self-analysis was going to fix anything. His issues stretched back decades. They were imprinted on the very marrow of his bones. This was a disaster. *He* was a disaster.

He knew he ought to ask her what was wrong, to see if there was anything he could do to help, but he didn't dare to in case she confirmed that he'd failed. Again. He didn't think he could bear to know that he'd made no progress at all, in spite of his best efforts, and most likely never would. What would that mean for him? For them? That, he couldn't bring himself to contemplate either.

'Do you want to go back?' was as much of a question as he would risk.

'No.' Her voice was thick, hoarse.

'Are you sure?'

'Yes. Just give me a minute. Please. I'll be fine.'

The nausea churned. He shifted on the seat. But he complied with her request because that, at least, he could do.

Zander had brought her to Lapland. He'd remembered a throwaway comment she'd made at the dinner with his siblings two nights ago when they'd been talking about dream holiday destinations, which in hindsight had been pretty surreal since the globetrotting bunch had all been pretty much everywhere already, and turned it into a reality.

Throat tight, eyes stinging, but not because of the biting cold that had hit her the minute she'd got off the plane, Mia swallowed hard, struggling to contain the tears that were threatening to fall.

She'd been a mess ever since he'd told her with that lethal smile where they were. For three hours he'd wrecked her physically and then he'd destroyed her emotionally. How many times had her cosmos-obsessed mother read her stories in books they'd taken out of the library about the magical place where the sun never set in summer and barely rose in winter? How often had they talked about one day actually making the journey to the Arctic to gasp in awe at the Northern Lights and to wish upon the stars?

It had never happened. There'd never been enough money or time, and once the dementia had sunk in its teeth, no one had been travelling anywhere. But even when her mother had been at her most confused and Mia at her most distressed, in her increasingly rare moments of lucidity she'd talked excitedly about when they would go, how they would get there and what they might do, and just for a while Mia had allowed herself to believe it, a beacon of light in the darkness, a flicker of hope in the desolation.

She missed her mother so much she felt as though her heart had been ripped from her chest. Her emotions had burst through the dam she'd built to contain them and were now rushing through her like a roaring river, so powerful, so strong that they crushed the air from her lungs.

She was filled with a bone-deep sense of loss. She ached with the agony of longing for things she'd never have. Such as this, the experience of a lifetime that she and her mother had dreamed of so often but had never got to share. Such as the maternal support and advice and the unique bond created by a child. The grandparent her child would never get to know.

But she couldn't collapse in a heap on Zander. This trip of his had been a lovely idea. She didn't want to ruin it for either of them, which she could tell she was in danger of doing because he was clearly thrown by her reaction. The tension and bewilderment radiated off him in waves.

So, as the sun emerged for its brief daily dalliance with the horizon, she took a deep breath and fought for control. Determinedly, she buried the grief that still had the power to blindside her when she least expected it and blinked back the tears. She focused on the landscape and let the beauty and serenity of the scenery sweep away the sorrow.

Thick snow lay on the ground and clung to trees that soared into the clear blue sky and cast long shadows. They passed through no villages, encountered no other vehicle, nothing but the dark green and blinding white forest for mile after otherworldly mile and the occasional glimpse of a reindeer.

Zander didn't ask her what was wrong. She supposed he didn't want to invade her privacy. But once she'd composed herself, she swallowed hard and told him anyway because she needed to clear the air.

'I'm sorry about that,' she said, her words sounding loud in the thick, swirling silence of the back seat. 'My mother and I planned this trip. We never got to make it. It threw me a bit. Sometimes I miss her so much it hurts.'

For a moment he said nothing. Then he let out a long, slow breath and his entire body relaxed. 'I had no idea.'

'Why would you?'

He took her hand and gave it a squeeze that she felt from head to toe. 'I know it's not the same,' he said gruffly, 'but you have my family now.'

And then he pulled her into his arms and gave her a kiss that was hot and hard and so full of *feeling* that her eyes started stinging all over again.

The glass and wood cabin at which they soon arrived was built on stilts, halfway up a hillside, nestled high amongst the trees. The driver took their bags up and then departed, leaving them utterly alone in this winter wonderland, but she didn't need anyone else. She just needed him.

However, since daylight in this part of the world at this time of the year was limited, they decided to save test driving the bed for later and take the snowmobile out for a spin instead.

'Do you know how to drive this thing?' Mia asked, only slightly reassured by the fact that she was so wrapped up in the thick winter clothing provided that if she did fall off at least her baby would be protected.

Zander stepped in close and put a helmet on her head. 'I do,' he murmured, taking his time as he did up the strap, brushing his fingers over what little skin was visible and making her shiver, deliberately, she suspected. 'Back in the day, before I took over the company and had more time, I spent a lot of time in the mountains. Skiing, snowboarding, I was up for anything.'

'Did you mind about having to give that up?'

'Not at all. I always wanted Leo's job. He was never happy in the role but clung onto it out of a misguided sense of duty until he met Willow and saw the light. I'm much better at it than he was.'

That remark, along with the wicked grin that accompanied it, made her heart flip with relief. She hadn't ruined anything. If anything, their connection felt closer and deeper than ever.

Reminding herself that she must not do anything else to spoil things, Mia hopped on the back of the two-person machine and clung on as Zander sped them through the eerily quiet wilderness and into a snowy canyon that featured a huge frozen waterfall so stunningly beautiful she wanted to weep. They had a drink in the fairy light lit restaurant of an ice hotel that was reconstructed every year, then he showed her how to drive the snowmobile and she took them back in the twilight, weaving through ancient pines and past picturesque lakes while he curled his big body around her, making her feel so protected, so safe that she didn't ever want it to stop.

Back at the cabin, they warmed up in front of a roaring fire that cast dancing golden shadows across the rugs. Zander assembled a late lunch while Mia stood at the huge picture window through which warm light spilled out and watched a pair of arctic fox cubs frolicking in the snow.

'Thank you for this,' she said over cheese baked into the shape of a pie and served with cloudberry jam and a bowl of *lohikeitto*, her smile soft, her throat tight, her heart thumping at twice its usual rate. 'And I don't just mean lunch. Today has been amazing.'

'You're very welcome.'

Later, lying in the huge bed next to him as he slept, naked beneath the silk sheets and cashmere blankets, she gazed up through the laser-heated glass roof at the aurora borealis painting the dark starlit sky with great swathes of glowing colours. The sheer scale and awesome majesty of what was going on overhead stole her breath and brought tears to her eyes all over again, and it was only when she thought that her mother would have loved this that she realised she'd stopped thinking about her mother hours ago.

From the moment she'd stepped out of the car all she'd thought about was Zander and this wonderful trip he'd arranged for her. Not for their baby or anyone else. For her. To please her and her alone.

He did care about her, she thought giddily. Possibly even more than that because he'd told her he'd never given anyone a present before, so this had to be special, surely. He was the most thoughtful, most amazing man she'd ever met. Not flawless—who was?—but deep and layered and complex. Her child was so lucky to have him as a father. She couldn't wait to see him caring for and playing with his son or daughter. She'd never had that experience with her own father, but she knew Zander was going to be great.

This was the most perfect Christmas present she could ever have been given, and as a shooting star streaked through the sky she knew that she didn't have to wonder any more about whether or not her heart was engaged. It was—wholly and irrevocably—because she was head over heels in love with him.

He was everything she'd always wanted. He'd talked to her, he trusted her, he valued her. He was the fairy tale. And she was pretty sure he loved her back. It was there in the tenderness of his touch. The warm heat of his smile. The faint trembling she'd felt in him when he'd kissed her in the car.

So what was she going to do about it? Wait to see how things panned out? That had never been her style. And how much of a risk would it really be to tell him how she felt? Surely it had to be minimal. Success, security, happiness, love—you had to reach out and grab them when you could. Because, as she well knew, life could simply be too short not to.

But a little voice in her head was telling her to exercise caution. These were early days still, and they'd been pretty intense ones at that. Only a fortnight ago Zander's life had changed for ever with the news that he, the tabloids' favourite international billionaire playboy, was going to be a father. Over the weekend everything he'd believed for the last thirty years had been tossed in the air and reshaped. It was a lot to contend with.

What if she dived right in and it was too much too soon? She did have form on that. What if, in the single-minded pursuit of her own happiness, she demolished his? If she told him how she felt and he spooked, definitely a possibility, how awkward would that be?

On this occasion, then, perhaps it would be

218 A CHRISTMAS CONSEQUENCE FOR THE GREEK

wise to wait. To test the waters first. She had to get it right. Her future, and their baby's, depended on it. She could not afford to screw it up.

Overall, it had been an extremely successful twenty-four hours, Zander thought with satisfaction as he made Mia a cup of green tea the following morning and took it back to her in bed.

Admittedly, the start had been shaky, but she'd explained what had happened and the relief that it hadn't been his fault, that his self-reflection hadn't been for naught, made him feel quite light-headed. The rest of the day had pleasingly played out as he'd envisaged—pure, exhilarating, carefree fun of the kind he hadn't had in a long time.

Zipping through the trees on the snowmobile first with Mia wrapped round him and then with him around her had given him more of a rush than any ski run, and he'd made it down La Chavanette intact, twice. Her delight at the ice hotel had been infectious. Her avid interest in the precise formation of the frozen waterfall another fascinating facet to discover.

He wasn't immune to the impact of the scenery either. More than once his breath had caught at the sheer magnificence of the landscape. Last night, he'd looked up at the canopy of stars and the swirling colours that danced across the sky and was perfectly willing to admit the sight had brought a lump to his throat.

There'd been something unique about making love beneath it. A new dimension to their heat. As if they'd somehow, impossibly, been trying to match up to the glory of nature. Mia's passion had been wild, her desire to please him infinitely more intense than usual. He still hadn't fully recovered.

'Can you believe it's Christmas Day in less than a week?' she said, taking the tea from him and snuggling back against the pillows. 'Scoffing jelly babies and watching old films in my pyjamas is going to be quite an anti-climax after this.'

'Is that what you usually do?'

'Yes.'

He frowned. 'On your own?'

'I know it doesn't sound much fun, but it's fine,' she said with a reassuring grin that strangely didn't reassure him at all. 'Really. I've had invitations over the years, but being part of other people's families only emphasises the fact that I don't have one. It's easier to treat it as just another day and I'm normally exhausted after the manic December rush anyway. There doesn't seem much point in going to a lot of effort when it's just me, and I've had more than enough of food by then. I don't even have the energy to put up a tree, let alone hang any decorations.'

She took a sip of her tea and he recalled her admitting to loneliness, thought about her breakdown yesterday morning, and found himself wishing he could remove her pain the way she'd removed his.

'What about you?' she said, pulling him away from that perplexing and faintly troubling notion and back to the conversation.

'Christmas isn't my favourite time of the year either,' he said. 'Neither of my parents was ever at home. My father was inevitably immersed in work. My mother was always somewhere hot and sunny. There wasn't a lot of festive spirit around. These days I have an open invitation to Leo's place on Santorini.'

'Is that what you're going to do this year?'

It was an idea. He never had before. He'd always felt as if he'd be intruding, so he tended to head to the office and then, when the eerie quiet got to him, which it inevitably did after a couple of hours, he walked the seven miles home and had an uncharacteristically early night. But this year, because of all the personal revelations he'd recently had and the implications of them, he could indeed buy some presents for his nieces and take them to Santorini.

'I'm undecided.'

'Well, I know that, technically, my two weeks will be up by then,' she said, her eyes shimmering as she looked at him from above the rim of her cup, 'but maybe we could spend the day together this year. Maybe we could start making some traditions of our own.'

The back of his neck prickled. His stomach pitched. But where his sudden discomfort came from, he couldn't say. It wasn't an outlandish suggestion because they could well be sharing many Christmases to come.

However, the sparkle in her gaze and the expression on her face unnerved him. She seemed to be radiating hope, warmth, yearning, and he couldn't work out whether all that was for his body or for something else.

Worse was the way in which his stomach was revolting at the thought of her moving out. Did she want to leave? Why? Wasn't she happy with their arrangement? He'd thought it was working well. He'd been thinking about making it permanent, for the sake of convenience.

But he didn't want to analyse the weird sense

of impending doom that was descending and settling over him like a weighted blanket. Or the disturbing feeling that he was suddenly on shaky ground. That could wait until they got back. This morning, as soon as the sun was up, they were heading out on a husky safari. No petrol fumes, no rumbling engines—just Mia and him and the call of the wild—and he wanted to enjoy it.

So he shoved aside the misgivings that he didn't understand, gave her a smile designed to disguise and said, 'Why not?'

It was six in the evening when they landed back in London. Encouraged by the events and conversations of the day, Mia asked Zander if they could take a detour to her flat en route to his apartment.

She could hardly contain her excitement as she riffled through the filing cabinet in the study area of her sitting room while he inspected the books on her shelves. To think that only a few short weeks ago she'd been all alone in this world, plodding along as she had for years, trying to carve out the future she wanted and so very lonely, and now here she was with a child on the way and the most gorgeous man in her life.

The signs that she'd been right about how he felt about her were all there. They were to spend Christmas Day together, the first, she hoped, of many. And the husky safari. What a ride that had been. He'd held her so close, so tightly. As if he never wanted to let her go. He hadn't missed an opportunity to touch her, to kiss her. And his smiles... Every single one of them spread through her like sunshine, warming the parts of her that had been so cold for so long.

If he'd been a fraction quieter on the flight back, a little withdrawn, a faint furrow between his brows, it had to be because he regretted the end of a wonderful two days. She could have stayed there for ever too.

'Aha.'

Having found what she wanted, Mia closed the drawer with a flourish, whirled round and held out a white rectangular envelope. 'Here,' she said, her heart skipping about all over the place, her breath catching in her throat. 'For you.'

He took it and frowned. 'What's this?'

'Open it.'

He did. He took out the document and unfolded it. Scanned it. And went very still. 'It's your birth certificate.'

'That's right,' she said, the adrenalin fizzing through her so powerful it made her head spin. 'The paperwork you requested. So we can get married.'

For a moment he didn't say anything, clearly too overwhelmed to speak, which was understandable because she was on the overwhelmed side too. It was an overwhelming moment.

But then he slowly folded the document back up and returned it to its envelope. He handed it back to her with a cool, 'Thanks, but no thanks,' and the excitement, the adrenalin, every good thing she'd been feeling instantly vaporised.

'Thanks, but no thanks?' she echoed, stunned, immobile, her breath catching at the sight of his now unreadable expression and a smile that did not spread warmth.

'I no longer see the need.'

What? She opened her mouth, found she had no words so closed it, then eventually managed a bewildered, 'Since when?'

'Since we started talking.'

'What about securing your rights?'

'The law is enough.'

'But you were so adamant.'

He gave a shrug. 'That came from a place of insecurity which, thanks to you, I no longer have.'

Mia didn't know what to say. This was not going the way she'd expected. She'd assumed he'd be delighted and whisk her off to the register office right then and there. It had never occurred to her that he might have changed his mind.

But she was not done. Because she'd been waiting for the right time to tell him how she felt and that time was now. 'What if *I* see the need?' she said, her voice tight, her pulse pounding in her ears. 'What if I *want* to marry you?'

'Do you?'

'Yes.' So much.

'I won't withhold access to my family, if that's what you're worried about. You'll have a generous allowance to use as you see fit. I'll buy you a house with a garden, of any description, wherever you wish. We don't need to marry to make this work. This isn't the nineteenth century.'

Those had been her words once, but not any more. What he was offering wasn't enough. It wasn't even the point. 'I don't want to marry you for the sake of our child,' she said, needing to clarify her desires and make him see what he clearly didn't. 'I want to marry you for no one's sake but *me*.'

'What do you mean?'

'I'm in love with you,' she said, unable to contain the feelings whipping about inside her like a Catherine wheel any longer. 'And you're in love with me.'

CHAPTER FOURTEEN

STANDING THERE IN the centre of Mia's small but cosy sitting room, Zander froze. Outside a car honked and someone shouted. Through the window he could see that the sun was shining and the sky was blue. In here, however, the silence thundered and the thick, heavy air crackled with the electrical charge of an approaching storm.

'That's absurd,' he said, denial slamming into every inch of him.

Mia gasped and recoiled as if winded, but nevertheless pulled her shoulders back and lifted her chin, which was inevitable because she'd never backed down from anything. 'Which bit of it?'

'All of it.' It had to be. How could it be anything else? 'You're doing what you said you wouldn't and reading something into this that simply isn't there. Apart from the baby, rampant lust with a side order of conversation is all we have.'

'You're being reductive.'

'I'm being honest.'

'No, you're not,' she said, her gaze fixing him to the spot. 'You introduced me to your family. You sought my opinion and advice and trusted me enough to share with me your deepest fears. You let me in. You *welcomed* me in. You took me to Lapland.'

Zander's jaw clenched. When she put it like that, he could see why she'd got the wrong idea. Her ridiculous assertion that they were in love with each other was a wholly unintended consequence of his desire to overcome the past in order to look forward to the future. Yes, they'd talked and developed a certain connection, but he'd been building a relationship, a practical arrangement that would lead to a smoother future, and that was it. Nothing more.

'As a thank you for helping me overcome my past.'

'You could have just taken me out to dinner.'

'I'd already done that.'

She folded her arms across her chest and arched one elegant red-gold eyebrow. 'So how do you explain the way you kissed me in the car on the way to the cabin?'

'That was merely sympathy.'

'We both know it was more than that,' she said with a sharp shake of her head. 'I felt you trembling.'

'With relief. Because I thought I'd got it wrong. I thought I'd failed. Again.'

'On the husky safari you held me in that sled as if you couldn't bear to let me go.'

'To stop you falling out and our baby coming to harm.'

'I was securely strapped in.'

Zander's words dried up. His head emptied. He had no counter-argument to that. What she said was true. They'd both been strapped in. And as it hit him that her other points were also true, his blood rushed to his feet and the ground surged up to reach him and he had to plant a hand on the bookcase to stop himself from passing out.

He could have taken her out to dinner. What he'd felt when he'd kissed her in the car hadn't just been sympathy and relief. He'd also ached with the need to draw out her pain and absorb it himself.

Which meant what? That he'd been lying to himself? No. He wasn't. He couldn't be. Because that would indicate that she was right and

230 A CHRISTMAS CONSEQUENCE FOR THE GREEK

they had something more than he'd assumed, which could not be the case.

He couldn't be in love with her, he thought, a cold sweat breaking out all over his skin. He was incapable of it. He'd got so good at burying his emotions, which had been abhorred by his father and ignored by his mother, and which he'd always considered so very dangerous, that he'd felt nothing deeply at all for years.

Except that ever since he'd met Mia he had.

Hurt, panic, confusion, relief, exhilaration, pride, terror—he'd felt them all, on occasion so profoundly, so volatilely that he'd staggered beneath their weight.

How many times had he tried to suppress them? Many. How often had he succeeded? Rarely.

She did mean something to him, he realised, his chest tight, his lungs constricting, the knuckles of the hand that was clutching the shelf whitening. She meant everything. And because of it, she had the power to destroy him. To trample all over his feelings, these new terrifying feelings that he hadn't even realised he had, and leave him there to bleed out, broken and hurting, a wreck.

But he couldn't have that. Such vulnerability was unacceptable. He would not put himself in a position where he could wind up weak and indecisive and doubting himself. He had to remain strong and steady and not slice himself open and offer her everything. He couldn't go there again and there'd been more than enough opening up already.

But it wasn't too late to retreat and pull up the drawbridge while he figured out how to fix what he'd done. All he had to do was take a deep breath and calm down and find a way through the chaos.

So, deploying the strategies that had worked so well for him so many times before, he shut down the cacophony in his head and switched himself off. A blessed numbness swept through him. Ice now flowed through his veins. And at last he could think clearly.

'Excuse me,' he said, wholly focused on the need to escape to safety and regroup. 'I need to go.'

The slam of her front door rang in her ears for hours, but although gutted that Zander hadn't swept her into his arms while confessing he loved her too, Mia wasn't entirely surprised that he'd hared off as if he had the hounds of hell at his feet. Spooking him with her declaration of love had always been a possibility. It wasn't the first time he'd retreated when feeling under threat. He'd frequently needed a moment or two to process information he'd been presented with.

The important thing was that she'd told him how she felt and made him aware of how she was certain he felt. The ball was now in his court, and with any luck it wouldn't take him too long to work things through and bat it back.

Until that happened she had plenty to occupy herself. She'd reacquaint herself with her flat, which seemed very small and cramped after eight days in his palatial apartment. She'd hunt around for a spare toothbrush and toothpaste since she'd left hers in her bag in his car. Then she'd work on the plans she'd conceived while staying with him. She'd been thinking of making Hattie a partner in the business. She'd soon need a lot of help and support, not to mention time off, and not only did she trust Hattie implicitly, her friend and colleague had earned it.

Giving him space would be tough and she'd miss him hugely, but she wasn't a teenager, pining by the phone. She could handle one night on her own. Her future and that of their child depended on her giving him space to come to the only conclusion there was, so the one thing she would *not* do was pressurise him.

However, after two days of complete radio silence, an increasingly confused and distressed Mia had to confront the fact that not only did Zander not intend to send anything back in the way of a ball, but also, he quite possibly wasn't even in the game.

What was taking him so long? she wondered worriedly as she deveined some prawns for tonight's drinks party for fifty with a peeling knife. Why did history seem to be repeating itself? Surely it was blindingly obvious how good they could be together.

Unless it wasn't, of course, and he couldn't think of anything worse.

Could that be it?

Had she somehow managed to get completely the wrong idea and pushed him away with her prodding and poking and the attempts she'd kept making to burrow beneath his surface? Had she put him under pressure to give her something he wasn't ready to give?

That had happened before.

Could it have happened again?

Her heart gave a quick lurch at the thought of it, the knife slipped and she nicked her finger. Berating her stupidity on more than one front, Mia abandoned the prawns, grabbed some kitchen towel and went in search of the first aid kit.

Had she really not learned *anything* from her previous relationships? Why had she had to say something? Why hadn't she been content with the status quo, with seeing how things played out, as she'd told herself she would on so many occasions?

But what if he'd *never* be able to give her what she truly wanted, which was him? she wondered, her hands trembling as she opened the box and hunted around for a plaster. What if he didn't love her? What then? She hadn't considered that possibility—one of many, it seemed, that had slipped her by—but now she had to. She had to accept the fact that she might well have taken a risk and lost.

And, God, it was as if that knife had sliced and diced her heart, so much did it hurt. Her eyes stung and a hot lump lodged in her throat.

If that *was* the case, how would she bear it?

What had she done?

And when he met someone else—or many someone elses, as he inevitably would—even if he didn't parade them in front of her and their child, she'd know they were there, and the thought of it was agony.

'The smallest cuts are the worst,' said Hattie, wincing in sympathy as Mia removed the kitchen towel pad and applied the plaster.

'You're absolutely right,' Mia replied, swallowing down that lump and snapping on a glove.

No doubt she was going to suffer a thousand of them. But she had to be strong because she couldn't just draw a line under everything and try to move on. At some point they were going to have to communicate, and if Zander wasn't going to initiate it, then she would.

But for that, she'd have to get her feelings under control so she wouldn't break down in front of him and beg him to forget she'd ever said anything, and that wasn't yet.

Three days after Zander had fled Mia's flat he'd fixed nothing and was no closer to working anything through.

They'd been the longest, most frustrating days of his life.

He couldn't concentrate. His appetite had dropped off a cliff. Unable to sleep at his apartment, which held too many damn memories, he'd taken up residence in the suite at his office, not that that had made any difference.

He didn't know which way was up. He was

scratchy and unreasonable. The minute he arrived at the office, his assistants scurried to hide.

And he hated it.

It wasn't him.

He'd had plenty of time to think about everything Mia had said. Certainly enough to admit
she was right. He *was* in love with her. He probably had been from the moment he'd laid eyes
on her. He'd spent weeks suppressing the memory of it, but when he'd taken her hand in her
unit on an east London industrial estate that
ordinary afternoon in June, he'd felt as though
he'd splintered apart and reformed differently.
Even if she hadn't got pregnant, he would have
eventually given in and sought her out.

He didn't want to be alone, he now knew,
he wanted her, but he just couldn't get past his
fears about vulnerability and potential destruc-
tion. He didn't know why. He'd tried to analyse
it, he'd even googled it, but to no avail.

Currently, Zander was not alone. He was
standing at the bar just off the ballroom of one
of London's top hotels, the venue for the company's Christmas party—not catered by Halliday Catering, thank God—downing whisky
like it was water.

He didn't want to be here. He was not in a
party mood. The noise generated by the chatter

of five hundred merry people and the thumping of the band was hurting his head. The trouble was, he didn't want to be anywhere else either. Being on his own, a situation in which there'd be no distraction from the utter hopelessness of his thoughts, certainly didn't appeal. In fact, he didn't know what he wanted. Apart from Mia. Who he couldn't have. And freedom from this horrible state of paralysis that meant he hadn't dealt with her belongings and, worse, hadn't been in touch.

Thalia, who was in attendance as head of the company's charitable foundation arm, joined him at the bar and ordered herself a glass of white wine. 'No Mia this evening?' she said, as if able to read his poor tortured mind.

His chest tightened. His head pounded. How much more of this could he take? 'Not tonight.'

'Nothing serious, I hope.'

His sister hoped in vain. And in the past he might have made light of it with a shrug and a smile, but tonight he didn't have the energy to put up a front.

'We're no longer together.'

'I didn't realise you had been in the first place.'

He knocked back the contents of his glass

and signalled for another. 'No, well, neither did I.'

'That's a shame.'

'It is.'

'Are you in love with her?'

'What makes you ask that?'

'You couldn't take your eyes off her at dinner last week. I honestly thought the room was going to go up in flames. Even Leo noticed.'

'I'm crazy about her,' he said, seeing little point in denying it when apparently it had been obvious to everyone but him.

'Does she love you?'

'So she says.'

'Then what's going on?'

He hadn't a clue. He hadn't a clue about anything any more. 'It's complicated.'

'You love her. She loves you. There isn't anyone else involved. What's complicated about that?'

If only it *were* that simple. But Thalia didn't fear having her heart ripped out and stamped all over.

'How do you do it?' he muttered, needing help like he'd never needed it before. 'How do you all do it?'

'Do what?'

'Embrace the love. How do you get past the

fear of it all going wrong and winding up in pieces?'

Thalia tilted her head in consideration for a moment. 'I guess you just have to weigh up the alternatives and then decide if the risk is worth taking.'

And therein lay the problem. His decision-making ability was history. The risk seemed insurmountable. But what *was* the alternative? A lifetime of misery and regret? Wanting Mia but not having her? Watching her gradually fall out of love with him and into it with someone else, as she inevitably would because she wasn't afraid to go for what she wanted?

Was that any way to live? Was that really the future he could see for himself? On the outside looking in? Letting her go out of cowardice? No. Absolutely not. Many things required a leap into the unknown. Not all of them ended in disaster. And why would she rip his heart out? She loved him. Or at least she had, three days ago.

'She told me she loved me and I walked out on her,' he muttered, sick at the memory of doing such a thing.

'Oh, dear.'

His gut churned with shame and remorse. 'I know.'

'Can you fix it?'

If he wasn't too late. If she hadn't given up on him. If she gave him a second chance. 'I hope so.'

The last thing Mia felt like doing at five in the afternoon was dropping by Zander's apartment in the cold and the dark to pick up the things she'd left behind. It was so final. So heartbreaking. And to make her do it on Christmas Eve? When they'd once planned to spend the following day together? She'd thought him many things, but never cruel.

Well.

She'd do this one last thing and draw a line under the last sorry fortnight. Chalk it up to experience and move on. They'd have to stay in touch, obviously, but not for months and she'd have got over him by then. Already her heart had begun to mend. A bit. Because did she really need someone in her life who scuttled off when the going got tough? No, she did not. Someone had to be the grownup in this relationship of theirs and it clearly wasn't going to be him.

But that was fine. As she'd told him weeks ago, she was perfectly capable of raising their child on her own. She had money. She didn't need Zander to buy her a house. She'd buy or rent one of her own when the time came. Her friends would be her baby's family. And if he still wanted to be involved, well, that was fine too. She could do cool. She could do detached. She'd take lessons from him.

But when she stepped out of the lift and strode into his apartment and saw what he'd done, she skidded to a halt, all her excellent intentions, her composure, her control, the very strength from her limbs just draining clean away.

Strings of fairy lights hung from every available point. Tasteful arrangements of foliage, pinecones and clove-studded oranges sat on almost every horizontal surface. A twelve-foot tree stood in one corner of the living room, swathed in garlands of lights and adorned with glass baubles. A fire crackled in the grate and innumerable flickering cinnamon-scented candles filled the air with the warm, spicy scent of Christmas.

Stunned into immobility, her heart shredded, Mia surveyed the scene, complete with carols softly emanating from somewhere and… Oh, no, she was going to cry again.

But she swallowed down the emotion, dug deep for cool detachment and turned to the man standing just to her left. 'If you could point me in the direction of my things,' she said with a bright, nothing-bothers-me smile that cost her everything she had, 'I'll be out of your hair in a jiffy.'

Zander started. Blinked, as if jolted out of a trance. 'What?'

'My belongings? I'm here to collect them.'

'Is that what you want?' he said, his brows snapping together in a deep frown.

No. Of course it wasn't what she wanted. She wanted him, so much still that she might as well not have bothered armour-plating her defences. He looked terrible, pale and drawn, but it did nothing to diminish his gorgeousness, which really wasn't fair when even though she'd spent hours on her hair, clothes and make-up—of which she was not proud—she still looked a mess. He was wearing a black shirt and faded blue jeans with nothing on his feet, and that wasn't fair either because he knew, because she'd told him, that she found that combination unbearably sexy.

She had to be so careful around this man. So very, very careful. Because if she let him, he could break her, for good this time.

'That's what *you* want.'

'No, it isn't,' he said. 'That was just a ruse

to get you here. I didn't think you'd come otherwise, after the last few days.'

Now it was Mia's turn to startle. 'Oh?'

'Why would I do all this if I didn't want you to stay?' he said, sounding a little wild, a little desperate. 'You were the one who mentioned creating new traditions.'

She reeled. Her heart lurched and then began to race. 'You did this for me?'

'Who else would I have done it for?'

'I don't know. Someone you've met in the last few days?'

'For six months, there's only been you, Mia,' he said, his dark eyes so intent on hers she could barely breathe. 'For the rest of my life there will always only be you. You even told me that.'

'At which point you walked out.'

'And I'll regret it for ever.' He took a step towards her and for one giddy moment she thought he was going to touch her, but then he stopped as if unsure whether that would be welcome. 'I'm so sorry about that. I was terrified of the strength of my feelings for you. Of how vulnerable they made me. I've spent years locking up my emotions. It was the only way I could handle my parents' neglect. Life just seemed easier and safer if I just didn't feel anything at all. But then I met you and that strategy went to hell in a handcart. You petrify and thrill me in equal measure, Mia. You could crucify me if you chose to, and that fear's taken a while to dispatch. But there is no one on this planet I would rather spend the rest of my life with. No one. I love you. You are the most magnificent woman I've ever met. I can't wait to meet our child and there is nothing more I'd like than to build a family with you. I want to give you everything. I want to make all your dreams come true.' He stopped, swallowed hard, then took a breath. 'If I didn't think there was a chance you might throw it back in my face,' he said gruffly, 'I'd start by giving you this.'

He dug a hand into the back pocket of his jeans and withdrew a small, square, black velvet box. And when he opened it with ever so slightly shaking hands, to reveal a blinding white diamond solitaire ring, despite all her attempts to remain cool and detached, the floor beneath her feet began to quake, sending shockwaves up through her body and cracking her heart wide open to spill love and joy and relief into every cell of her being.

She had no defence against this man who could crucify her too but wouldn't, because why would they do that to each other when theirs was a love strong enough to withstand whatever life had to throw at them? No defence at all against the tsunami of feeling rushing through her, which made her chest swell with such happiness she thought she would burst.

'I wouldn't throw it back in your face,' she said, perilously close to tears again.

He stilled. A light began to shimmer in those wonderful dark eyes of his. 'No?'

'I'd wear it every day.'

Barely before she'd finished her sentence he stepped forward and yanked her into his arms, kissing her so hard and for so long she saw stars. He tangled his hands in her hair, holding her close, murmuring things in Greek that she didn't technically understand but nevertheless did because they were so passionate they could only be words of love.

'I thought I'd ruined everything,' he muttered when at last he lifted his head, looking dazed, breathing hard.

Mia leaned back in his arms, looked around the room so thoughtfully, so stunningly transformed and shot him a smile. 'The decorations were a good move.'

'I hoped they would be.'

'And, as proposals go, an engagement ring certainly beats a birth certificate.'

'I thought that too.' He took her left hand and threaded his fingers through hers and brought it up to the gap that separated his heart from hers. 'Would you like to put it on now?'

She looked down at their joined hands, knowing they'd be united for ever, so excited to see what the future would bring, and said softly, 'I can't think of anything I'd like more.'

EPILOGUE

One year later

'A LITTLE TO the left,' said Mia, tilting her head from side to side and narrowing her eyes. 'No. That's too far. A fraction to the right… Perfect.'

Zander, who had been up a ladder, stepped down off it, set it to one side and then returned to the bed, where she lay with their six-month-old son, Toby, who was asleep, starfished across her chest.

The mattress dipped as he sprawled himself beside her and surveyed his handiwork. 'I can see why Willow didn't think it suitable for public display.'

So could Mia. The portrait was of the two of them, fully clothed, arranged on a bench in the garden beneath a blossoming apple tree. There was nothing untoward about the pose, but they were gazing at each other in such adoration, the chemistry between them so strong it was almost tangible, that they might as well have been naked. The only place it could hang was in their bedroom. 'She said she had to switch on the fan in her studio to cool herself down the first few times she worked on it.'

'You look as if you want to devour me.'

'You look as if you just *have* devoured me.'

'I had, if I recall correctly,' he mused with the beginnings of a smile that always meant trouble. 'It's giving me ideas.'

Her heart skipped a beat. Desire stirred. 'Ideas, huh?'

'Hold that thought.'

While Zander gently lifted their son off her and went to settle him in the nursery, Mia held that thought, along with a million others that she had to pinch herself every day to believe.

So much had happened in the last twelve months. They'd married in spring and, after a two-week honeymoon in Tahiti, had moved into this six-bedroomed house with a garden in the leafy London suburb that buzzed with cafés and parks. Hattie had become a partner in the business soon after that and in the summer Toby had been born.

Gone were the shadows and loneliness of the past. Zander now found family gatherings a joy and she had all the love and security she'd ever wanted. He'd promised to give her everything, to make her dreams come true, and he had. He'd given her the fairy tale.

'Now, where were we?' he murmured, strolling back into the bedroom and letting his gaze drift over her so thoroughly, so leisurely that she burned.

'You were having ideas.'

'So I was.'

He lowered himself onto the bed and she welcomed him into her arms and they explored and expanded on his ideas until they collapsed into a breathless heap of thundering hearts and tangled limbs.

And when the clock struck twelve and he murmured, 'Happy Christmas, *agàpi mou*,' Mia knew that it absolutely was.

* * * * *

Swept up in the festive magic of
A Christmas Consequence for the Greek?
You'll definitely enjoy the first instalment in
the Heirs to a Greek Empire trilogy,
Virgin's Night with the Greek!

In the meantime, dive into these
other stories by Lucy King!

The Secrets She Must Tell
Invitation from the Venetian Billionaire
The Billionaire without Rules
Undone by Her Ultra-Rich Boss
Stranded with My Forbidden Billionaire

Available now!